ADVANCE PRAISE

National news media reports 8 dead and 14 "non-life threatening injuries" at the terrorist attack at Starbucks.

Seriously! Paralysis is a non-life threatening injury?

What an impactful way to begin a story! How many of us currently live in fear of another terrorist attack—one that might well involve us? ISIS is a word bandied about daily... almost to the point of having become one with our culture. Terrorism. Really? One questions the why and comes away empty-handed.

However, lest I get carried away with what is only the root of another of Don Wooldridge's creative manuscripts, let me say he has done an amazing job of switching from his barter trilogy... to his courageous journey of Bipolar II Disorder... to an exciting, twisting story that does touch each of our lives today. His walk through the trauma of a terrorist attack and its impact on a young couple just embarking on life is so rich, so real.

As usual, Don's characters live and breathe on the pages; his research into the Ft. Collins location and the medical aspects of spinal damage all bring creative reality to the intrigue and surprises readers find in the pages of another great book. Another great work of turning life into fiction!

~T R Stearns
Retired School Superintendent

BROKEN DREAMS

National news media reported 8 dead
and 14 "non-life threatening injuries"
at the terrorist attack at Starbucks.

Seriously! Paralysis is a non-life threatening injury?

By

Don Wooldridge

D & PW Publishing
ISBN-13: 978-0692843819 (Custom Universal)
ISBN-10: 0692843817
BISAC: Fiction / Romance / Action & Adventure

Also available in Digital

Printed in the United States of America
10 9 8 7 6 5 4 3 2 1

Cover design by Patrick Sipperly

Editing, formatting and interior design by Voices in Print Publishing

DEDICATION

To all the men, women and children who have survived a mass murder or a terrorist's attack, and who's trauma, injuries, and personal loses were brushed off by the media as a non-life threatening injury.

TABLE OF CONTENTS

ACKNOWLEDGEMENTS

This novel would not have been possible without the interest and assistance of family and friends. A special thank you to Kenny Hosack, the Director of Public Relations for Craig Hospital, Englewood, Colorado, who gave valuable time and expertise to the development of *Broken Dreams*.

BROKEN DREAMS

National news media reported 8 dead
and 14 "non-life threatening injuries"
at the terrorist attack at Starbucks.

Seriously! Paralysis is a non-life threatening injury?

By

Don Wooldridge

CHAPTER 1

The soaring snow-capped Rocky Mountains provide the backdrop for Fort Collins, Colorado. A large sign reading, "Children's Activity Center" hangs on a modern one-story building. Parents and children pass in and out of the main entrance.

Tyler Daly, 30, was dressed as a clown and standing on a small stage performing magic tricks in front of a crowd of kids and their parents.

"Can I have a couple of volunteers to help me with my next trick?"

A number of kids raised their hands and jumped up and down. Tyler pointed to a girl and a boy.

"You two… come on up!"

The girl and boy ran up onto the stage. Tyler leaned down and peered closely at the little girl.

"Are you hiding that from your mother?"

The little girl smiled and shrugged, befuddled. Tyler reached behind the girl's ear and pulled out a quarter.

The girl giggled. Tyler turned to the boy.

The boy hesitated. "I don't have any quarters behind my ears!"

Tyler looked at the audience.

"He's right! He doesn't have any quarters!"

He slipped his hand behind the boy's ear and pulled out a rolled up dollar bill. The audience laughed and clapped as he unrolled the dollar and displayed it for the audience to see.

Back in his dressing room, still dressed in his clown costume, Tyler was texting a message on his phone when the center's Director walked into the room.

"Great show, Tyler! I don't know who enjoys you more the kids, the parents or me and the staff!"

"Thanks. It's always a blast." Tyler got up to leave. "I'm sorry but I need to get going. I'm meeting my… my friend, Abby."

The Director looked at Tyler and said, "You're not going to change into street clothes?"

Tyler smiled. "Absolutely not. The fun has just begun!"

He hurried out as the Director frowned, puzzled.

Still in his clown apparel Tyler was sitting behind the wheel of his car. He pulled the rearview mirror around to check himself out.

Perfect!

As a clown he was waving at other drivers and smiling at their double takes. The kids who were riding in their parent's cars waved and laughed at him. He caused quite a stir and enjoyed the show as much as the people who saw him.

Reaching the Starbucks Coffee Shop, Tyler pulled his car into the parking lot, parked and opened the trunk. He tugged and tugged until he was finally able to pull his red nose off. He took a tissue and wiped his clown make-up off.

Got most of it. Abby will understand.

Tyler pulled his clown suit off, wearing a T-shirt and jeans underneath it. He threw his costume into the trunk.

Then he leaned against the car and pulled his large clown shoes off and threw them into the trunk. He slipped into his athletic shoes and hurried into Starbucks.

***

Abby Porter, 29, a tall beautiful redhead was poring over the screen of her laptop.

The buzzing of Abby's phone drew her attention away from her computer and tomorrow's news article. Glancing quickly, she read a text massage.

"Can you meet me at Starbucks at 10? It's important."

It was Tyler. Nobody else got her to action quicker than Tyler Daly, her friend and confidant since childhood. She looked at the clock to see she needed to leave right away, to be there by ten. She sent a quick text "Sounds good," and picked up her purse and keys to leave. As she started to head out she ran right into Gus Odem, her fifty-year-old editor and boss.

"Oops."

"And where do you think you're going? We have a hard deadline coming up, Abby."

"I'm going on a break, Gus. Kind of a normal thing. And I'm well aware of my deadline."

"What about your article?"

Abby took a few steps back from Gus, turned and then started to walk off.

"My article is almost perfect, Gus. After I get back, I'll tweak it a bit and then it will be beyond perfect."

"I have to have it before noon for it to make tomorrow's issue!"

"Not a problem . . . Do I ever disappoint, Gus?"

Gus glanced at her open laptop computer.

"The article's on your laptop?"

"Yeah . . . why do you ask?"

"Just want to get to it in case, you know, you get hit by a bus."

Abby looked at Gus disapprovingly and shook her head. "So glad you're concerned . . . about the article. Look, Gus, nothing is going to stop me from coming back to finish up my piece and turning it in on time!"

On her way to Starbucks, Abby rolled the window down allowing the wind to play with her long red hair. She smiled, thinking back to their elementary school days in Fort Collins, Colorado, and remembered...

She was a skinny eight-year-old tomboy with freckles to match her ginger hair, running in the playground with two other girls. She paused when she spotted Tyler, then nine and a bit shorter than she, sitting on the bench by the schoolyard, reading a book.

Abby walked over to him.

"What are you reading, Tyler?"

Tyler looked up surprised to see Abby standing before him. Abby's two friends walk up behind her. "A book."

Abby smiled and shook her head. "What's it about?"

"Insects."

Abby made a face. "Eeeew! I hate bugs."

"I love' um."

Sally, who was standing beside Abby said, "He would! Come on, Abby. Let's play hide and seek."

"Tyler, you wanna play?" Abby asked.

Disinterested, Tyler said, "I'd rather read."

"You know you're kinda boring?"

He looked up at Abby. "Yeah, that's what everyone says."

One more time Sally says to Abby, "Come on Abby, let's play. Tyler's boring."

Tyler smiled at Abby, "See, told you."

Abby looked at Tyler, her eyes soft, sympathetic.

There was a reason Tyler was reserved, and Abby knew why. She flashed back to that awful day in the funeral home.

Abby, 8, walked up to Tyler, 9, and his mother, Mary, 35, who were standing in front of a casket. Abby took Tyler's hand.

"Sorry, about your father."

He kept looking into the casket, but said, "That's okay. Wasn't your fault."

"I'm still sorry."

Mary embraced Abby, as tears ran down her face. "Abby, I have to get a job now… your mother's going to watch Tyler after school. Tyler loves you like a sister… always watch out for him, Abby. Please! Always watch out for Tyler."

Abby's thoughts drew a few traces of tears in her eyes, despite the breeze through the open car window. In almost a whisper Abby repeated those words again. "Always look out for Tyler."

CHAPTER 2

Tyler was sitting at a small table in Starbucks, fidgeting, as he waited for Abby. Every time the door swung open he craned his neck hopeful that Abby was entering. Impatient, he decided to go ahead and order.

As the barrister handed him two coffees, Abby suddenly appeared behind him.

She got close to his ear and said, "If one of those is for me it better be a *vente* latte!"

Tyler turned and smiled widely at Abby who grimaced slightly.

"What?" Tyler asked in reaction to her concerned look.

She tried to rub a smudge off his face, saying, "I see you were doing your clown thing today."

"Oh, I didn't get all the make-up off?"

"I can still see the little blue stars under your eyes and the large red outline around your lips."

"Guess I was in a hurry."

Abby took her coffee from Tyler and they moved to a table. "I'll get you some make-up remover for your birthday."

Tyler shook his head at the remark. "Oh, great."

Abby asked, "What was the important thing you wanted to talk about? My editor is ready to kill me for leaving."

"Let's have a seat."

They sat across from one another. "So what's up?"

He sipped his coffee, then stared at the cup. "You know, you have it all, Abby. You're smart, socially involved, and physically fit... not to mention sexy and beautiful."

Abby cocked her head and looked intently at Tyler. "Tyler, have you been drinking?"

"Just coffee. Look, I've always been slightly intimidated by you. I know I don't measure up."

"Now, don't be ridiculous. You know you've been my life-long hero. I hate to interrupt this tribute to me... but I haven't got much time. My article on the Swetsville Zoo is going to be featured on the Life & Style page and..."

"All right, all right! Well, listen, I've been hired by the University of Texas in Austin to be a computer system's supervisor."

"Congratulations."

"I want you to come down with me."

Setting her cup down she smiled, "Sure. Whatever I can do. You want me to drive your car down or drive a U-Haul for you?"

Tyler leaned closer to Abby. "Abby, I love you."

Abby cocked her head to one side and smiled warmly. "Love you, too, Bro!"

"No... I mean I'm in love with you."

Abby was speechless.

"I want you to come with me. I love you and want to marry you. Will you marry me?"

Abby's eyes grew wide with surprise. Just as she opened her mouth to respond their table trembled and the floor seemed to move beneath them as a loud explosion was heard.

The windows of the coffee shop blew out. Glass shards shot everywhere like high-speed bullets. There were screams and moans of pain from patrons and employees who were injured.

Abby screamed as she looked down at her arm that was filled with glass shards. "Oh, my God! What's happening?"

Suddenly, two men with masks covering the lower portions of their faces entered the coffee shop. They shouted "*Allahu Akbar*! *Allahu Akbar*!" They then started firing their semi-automatic rifles.

The gunmen sprayed a barrage of ammo all around the coffee shop. People screamed in pain as they were hit. Some collapsed and were dead before they reached the floor; others suffered differing degrees of injury.

Tyler screamed in agony and dropped to the floor. Abby pulled a tipped-over table closer for her and Tyler to hide behind it.

Some patrons and employees raced past Tyler and Abby into the restrooms to take cover. Abby's heart was in her throat when, from her prone position, she saw the boots of someone walk up and stand beside their table.

The gunman walked on and entered the restroom, which he sprayed with a vicious barrage of gunfire to the wails and screams of the people who thought they were safe there.

After a final flourish of gunfire, the gunman in the main room stopped, hearing the blare of multiple sirens that were growing increasingly louder he shouted, "We need to go! Now!"

9

The gunman who was in the restroom rushed out; Abby saw him run by as she crouched on the floor, her body covering Tyler's. She watched as the two gunmen left the coffee shop filled with the moans and sobs of the injured and terrified.

Abby whispered, "I... I think they're gone. Tyler, are you okay?"

"I don't know. My leg was hit and hurts like the devil. I was hit in the back and it really stung but now I don't feel anything."

"Hang in there... help is on the way."

The sirens drew ever closer.

Tyler laid his head on Abby's lap as she stroked his hair. Abby looked at Tyler. She grimaced at his wounded leg, which was bleeding profusely. She used napkins that had fallen on the floor, to try to stem the bleeding. She cried out of frustration... she couldn't stop the bleeding.

"Where are the cops?"

Abby peeked up over the turned over table that had saved their lives. Tears streamed down her face as she scanned the coffee shop, devastated by the carnage of the dead, the dying and the injured.

"Help! Help! Help us!"

The sounds of the door opening and many footsteps at first frightened Abby. She freaked out when Sergeant Jim Scott, appeared, wearing a riot helmet and bent over the table. He saw that Abby was terrified.

"We're friends. Here to help. Sergeant Scott, SWAT Team."

Sergeant Scott pulled the visor of his helmet up so that Abby could see him.

She told him, "I'm okay. But he—Tyler..." Abby gestured towards Tyler.

Breathlessly, Tyler tells him, "I'm alive. My leg... I got hit... hit in the leg. But it doesn't hurt."

Sergeant Scott righted the table and shoved it aside. Other police officers, uniformed cops and plainclothes detectives, were walking all about the coffee shop looking in doors, under tables, everywhere. The uniformed cops led with their assault rifles and were ready to strike.

Sergeant Scott bent down by Tyler as he talked into the microphone attached to his shoulder. "Medical support. Man down... gunshot wound, heavy bleeding."

Then, Sergeant Scott peered closely at the area around Tyler's back. He said almost to himself, "Where's all that blood coming from?"

"His leg?" Abby asks.

"It's pooling around his back."

Sergeant Scott turned Tyler gently over on his side. Blood was pouring out of a gunshot wound on his back. Sergeant Scott pulled Tyler's shoe off in an instant and gave his big toe a pinch.

"Can you feel that?"

Tyler looked up. "Feel what?"

Sergeant Scott turned to speak into his shoulder microphone again. "Urgent. Need Medevac transport from crime scene. Victim down, gunshot wound in the leg and potential SCI injury."

Abby looked scared to death. "What's that? What's an SCI injury?"

Sergeant Scott addressed Abby quietly. "Spinal cord injury."

Tyler looks up plaintively at the police officer. "Are you saying I'm... I'm paralyzed? No wonder I can't feel anything."

Abby's tears start up again.

"I'm not a doctor but your wounds need immediate attention."

Tyler yelled in frustration, "I don't want to live if I'm paralyzed. Shoot me now, please, Sergeant, shoot me now!"

Through her sobs Abby says, "Tyler, don't even say that!"

"Look at it this way," Sergeant Scott said to Tyler, "the terrorists tried to kill you and failed. There are a lot of dead people in here. You were saved for some reason. You have to live to find out what that reason is."

Tyler was stunned by Sergeant Scott's words and traumatized by the incident and his injuries. Abby grabbed Tyler's hand but was too choked up to talk. Moments later, EMT Techs rushed in with a gurney, assessed his injuries, lowered the stretcher, rolled Tyler gently onto a transfer mat and lifted him carefully onto the gurney. The techs secured him, raised the gurney back up and rushed off with him.

Abby jumped up and started to leave. "I'm going with him."

Sergeant Scott gently grabbed her arm. "You can hurry and say your good-byes. But you need to come back and be treated here. Your arm is full of glass. They can take care of you here."

Abby was torn between going and staying. "Where are they taking him?"

"Wherever he can get the best treatment. I don't know where that is at this moment. Now, run and tell him goodbye; then come back. The detectives need to talk to you. You were an eyewitness to a mass murder." Sergeant Scott glanced around at the carnage, his face stoic and said, "to a massacre."

Abby stared at Sergeant Scott. He waved her on, saying, "Go!" She turned and took off running after Tyler. She was holding Tyler's hand as she ran alongside the fast moving gurney being guided by the techs towards the back of the EMT vehicle.

"Tyler, you're going to be fine. The hospital, the doctors, they'll take care of you."

He looked up and squeezed her hand. "Abby, come with me."

"I can't. I have to give a statement to the police."

"I'm afraid, Abby."

"So am I."

Abby was forced to let go of Tyler's hand as he was slid into the EMT van.

"Tyler"

"Abby"

"I'll find you, Tyler. I'll find you."

CHAPTER 3

Tears streamed down Abby's face as she watched the EMT van drive off, sirens blaring and lights flashing.

Later, her arms were wrapped in gauze, and a few spots of blood seeped through the bandages as a female reporter approached her.

"I'm writing an article on the terrorist's attack. Looks like you were a victim."

Abby just looked at her, remaining silent.

"The reporter continued, "Do you feel fortunate that your injuries weren't serious?"

Abby's eyes narrow in anger. "The word "fortunate" is inappropriate for any part of what... what took place here. I wasn't injured badly but my best friend was, along with I don't know how many others."

"Did you see anyone killed? Did you hear the wails of the injured and dying?"

Abby was irritated. "It seems you're eager to get to the blood and guts of the matter."

The reporter shrugged, saying, "That's today's journalism."

"Look, what happened here... for me is personal. They are my memories, my experiences. I plan to share them with my readers."

The reporter backed up a step, said, "Sorry... I didn't realize you were a reporter," and walked away.

Amid the chaotic activity Abby spotted an open doorway at the back of Starbucks. She looked all around, from side to side, and then hurried to the door. She looked inside and smiled. Her purse was lying on the floor only a few feet away. Abby started to enter the door.

"Young lady!" a policeman yelled.

Abby stopped in her tracks. The police officer walked up to her.

Innocently she says, "Were you talking to me?"

He scowled at her. "Guilty conscience?"

Abby pointed through the doorway. "Look inside there. My purse with my keys, my phone, credit cards, money... my whole life is just inches away."

The police officer stood in front of the doorway with his arms across his chest, shaking his head "no."

"Oh, come on. I'm a reporter. I'd love to write a human interest story about how cops like you saved so many lives and brought us comfort and safety."

"Don't try to butter me up!" the policeman said. Pointing to a gurney, he said, "Getting your purse is way down on the priority list here."

Abby followed where he was pointing and saw an injured little girl who was being carried away by EMT techs.

She softened her attitude and said, "You have a good point."

The policeman escorted her away from the doorway.

A while later Abby was standing with a plainclothes detective who was writing on a small notepad. The reporter who approached Abby earlier walked up and stood a short distance away, trying to overhear the conversation.

"Did you get a good look at the gunmen?" The detective asked Abby.

"I only saw one of them. I actually first saw his boots. Later I saw him from a distance. He was dressed all in black and he was wearing a mask that covered everything but his eyes."

"Did you hear him talk? Did he have an accent?"

"It was foreign... not sure from where. Maybe the Middle East."

The detective made a few final notes. "Okay. If you think of anything, contact us. We may want to talk again."

Anxious to connect with Tyler, she asked, "Do you know where they're taking the injured?"

The detective scanned the area before he relied. "It's chaos central here. The techs don't know where they're going with the injured until they get in the ambulance and are told where to take their patients."

The detective seemed nice and helpful. Abby decided to try again. "Detective, can I get my purse? It's just inside..."

He shook his head abruptly. "It's a crime scene."

Disappointed she said, "I know... I lived it. I don't have anything. No money, no car keys... can't I just sneak back in there and get my purse? What harm could it do?"

"It's restricted to anyone other than police and fire personnel."

"Well, that just makes a bad day worse. Can you sneak in and get it for me?"

In spite of Abby's desperation the detective was still shaking his head. "I can only go into the crime scene on official business. I don't think getting your purse qualifies."

A tech rolled a gurney with a dead victim by. Abby and the detective looked at the deceased as it passed them. The detective turned and looked intensely at Abby.

"You have to remember how lucky you are."

The detective walked off. Abby sighed as she watched the injured being tended to and the dead being carted away. The police were done with her and there was no hope of her getting into the building. So, Abby started to leave the Starbucks parking lot on foot, when the reporter hurried over to her.

"Couldn't get your purse, huh?"

Abby just looked at the reporter and kept walking.

The reporter kept pace with her. "Don't tell me you have to walk home. I tell you what, if you agree to let me write your story, I'll give you a ride home."

Abby stopped, turned and looked at the reporter face-to-face and said, "Well, then... it looks like I'm hoofing it!"

As Abby turned to go the reporter had a frown on her face.

Walking down the streets of Fort Collins she mumbled to herself, "I wish we could go back to a simpler time."

About twelve years ago I was leading the cheerleading squad at a high school football game. I spotted Tyler walking onto the field, smiled and waved at him. Tyler was so embarrassed he turned red from ear to ear.

Because Tyler was shorter than the athletes he was standing behind, he couldn't watch the game from the sidelines or cheer on his Teammates.

An assistant coach walked up to Tyler and asked, "Hey, son, why don't you stand in front of some of these taller guys so you can see."

Tyler had a bird's eye view of the cheerleaders, and me so he said, "Actually, coach, I'm in a perfect spot. I can see just fine."

The assistant coach shrugs and walks off.

Abby giggled at the thought, but was drawn to reminisce about Tyler's true talents.

Tyler was 19 when he performed with the local symphony. He was featured on the piano.

When he received a standing ovation there were tears of pride and joy in my eyes.

Standing with the orchestra conductor after the performance Tyler spotted me and motioned me over to them and introduced me.

"Sir, this is Abby Porter.

The conductor smiled and said, "You didn't exaggerate about how pretty she is."

I smiled and blushed.

The conductor asked, "I take it you're... uh... a member of the family?

"No sir," Tyler interjected, "I'm an only child and since my mother passed away... Abby is my family."

I remember putting my arm around Tyler's shoulders. "I'm like his sister, sir. Only closer. We always look out for each other.

Tyler smiled widely and looked adoringly at me.

"We do, don't we?"

"Always..." I replied.

Tyler looked at the conductor, "She has a way of making everything better for me."

CHAPTER 4

Reaching her apartment without keys or personal identification, Abby came back to reality abruptly. She was embarrassed to beg for the super's help but had no choice, and knocked on his door. A few moments later, Glenn, the sixty-two-year-old building superintendent, opened the door. There was a scowl on his face.

"If you have a complaint, send me an e-mail." Glenn started to shut the door, but Abby pushed against it.

"Wait! I don't have my keys."

"Again?" he asked.

"Come on! That must be someone else! I've never lost them before! This is the first time I've ever asked you to open my door for me!"

Glenn looked greatly annoyed. "Hopefully it's the last!"

Abby rolled her eyes.

In disgust Glenn said, "Wait here!"

He stepped back inside. A few moments later he emerged with a set of keys as big as his fist. "All right let's go. I've got work to do."

Glenn led the way to Abby's apartment. Abby had to hurry to keep up with him.

"You young people lose way more keys than our older residents."

"I didn't lose my key, Glenn. I was in the terrorist attack at the Starbucks. My keys are locked up at the crime scene."

Glenn looked at Abby and shook his head. "I gotta hand it to you young people. You sure come up with the most outlandish excuses."

"Look! My arm is bandaged?"

Glenn noticed but didn't care. "Nice touch!"

"You know I don't care what you think, Glenn. I just want to get in my apartment."

They arrived at Abby's apartment and Glenn unlocked the door.

"Here you go... If you need another key, it'll cost you. I'll put it on your monthly statement."

"Whatever..."

Abby opened the door. "I hope I don't have to bother you again."

Glenn turned to leave saying, "Not as much as I do."

Abby shut the door, kicked her shoes off and plopped on the couch. "What a day!" Where are you when I need you, Tyler?

Abby sat up abruptly.

Yeah...where are you?

Abby quickly walked over to her PC, logged on, input some data and waited for the results. She peered at the screen. Her shoulders slumped.

Twelve hospitals in the area! He could be at any one of them.

Abby picked up her desk phone and dialed one of the phone numbers that was displayed on the screen.

When there was an answer she said, "Yes, I'd like to know if Tyler Daly has been admitted there."

She paused, listened. "He... he was injured in the terrorist shooting... yes at Starbucks."

She paused and listened again. "You can't release the names yet?"

Abby looked forlorn as she clicked off the phone. But undeterred she continued her search for Tyler. The apartment was dark, illuminated only by a dim desk light and the monitor. Abby peered at her computer screen as she made another call.

"I'm looking for Tyler Daly."

Again she paused and listened.

"He was in the shooting…"

She listened, "Okay, thanks any way. No one else could tell me either."

CHAPTER 5

Abby suffered an anxious sleepless night, tossing and turning The whole night was about Tyler. As soon as she awoke, even before dressing, Abby was on the phone calling hospitals. Finally, she found him on her sixth call. He had been admitted to the Poudre Valley Hospital on Lemay Avenue, about four miles from her apartment.

Abby was delighted; she had found him. Showering, dressing, and gulping down a cup of coffee she instinctively reached for her purse as she headed for the door.

Damn, I don't have it, and I need money.

Shaking her head in frustration she slipped her messenger bag over her shoulder, and began walking the four long miles to the hospital. She had no idea if her story was printed or not, so she stopped at a newspaper stand to peer through the glass door. It was fruitless since all she could see was the front-page pictures and headline about the attack on Starbucks.

When Abby reached The Poudre Valley Hospital she saw a beehive of activity. Scores of visitors, patients and professional staff members continually entered and left through the main entrance.

Abby walked toward the entrance looking with awe at the large medical center.

Once inside she found the lobby was as busy, matching the traffic at the main entrance. Abby approached the receptionist.

"Excuse me Ma'am. What room is Tyler Daly in?"

The receptionist looked at her computer screen, inputting some data.

"He's in ICU. Only family members are allowed to see him. Are you a family member?"

Abby hesitated, "Uh..."

Looking up at Abby and raising her eyebrows the receptionist asked, "Sister... cousin?"

Abby hesitated again, "Uh..."

The receptionist grinned, saying, "I know you're not his mother."

Finally, Abby found the words she needed. "Thank you for that. I'm his... uh... fiancée."

The receptionist craned her neck looking at Abby's left-hand.

"Oh, my ring."

"I don't see it, dear. Shouldn't you have one?"

"I know. We were in the terrorist attack yesterday. The ring is in my purse, which I can't get to because it's part of the crime scene.

"Hmm... if you can have it by tomorrow..."

Abby felt a bit of hope in the air and responded, "Oh, yes. I'm sure I can."

"Okay, then. You can see him today... He's in Intensive Care on the fourth floor."

"Thank you so much!" Abby said as she darted off to the elevators.

Oh My God! I can't believe how easily I lied. Where am I going to find an engagement ring before tomorrow?

Abby got off the elevator and walked slowly down the eerily quiet fourth floor. Nurses, doctors and other staff moved silently, apparently out of respect for the very ill patients on the floor. She was cautious; afraid she might disturb someone.

Jeremy, a thirty-two-year-old male nurse, spotted Abby and walked up to her. He spoke in quiet tones.

"Can I help you, Miss?"

"Yes. I'm here to see Tyler Daly? I'm... I'm his fiancée."

Jeremy smiled widely. "My name is Jeremy, and Tyler is one of my patients."

Abby felt some relief. "How's he doing?"

"He made it through surgery just fine but he's still under."

Abby's anxiety increased as she sensed the concern in Jeremy's comment. "Is that normal?"

"The doctors are keeping him in a medically-induced coma so he doesn't move and heals faster. You want to see him?"

"I do but... I'm afraid, too."

"Don't be. It'll help him for you to be there."

Abby got a determined look on her face and stood up tall. Trying to put her fears behind her she told Jeremy, "Okay. I'm ready."

Jeremy took a few steps toward one of the rooms and slid open the door. He gestured for Abby to enter.

27

Abby tentatively walked up to the room and stepped in.

"Jeremy smiled and said, "I'll let you two be alone."

He closed the door behind him as he left the room.

Abby's eyes were wide with fear and confusion as she looked at all the tubes, IVs, devices and monitors that Jeremy was hooked up to. She was overwhelmed by the whooshes and swishes that continuously emanated from the equipment.

Just then the door opened and a man in his fifties entered the room.

"Abby?"

Startled, Abby turned around.

"I'm Tyler's physician, Dr. Ingram. Jeremy told me you were in here."

Still shaken by his sudden appearance, she reply came out as a question, "Yes, sir?"

"I know you're scared, but Tyler is a strong, healthy young man and made it through his surgery with flying colors."

Abby's eyes are filled with tears of joy. "Then, he's going to be okay?"

Dr. Ingram lowered his eyes for a moment, and then looked back up at Abby.

"He is going to live. However, at this point... there is a strong possibility that the prognosis will be paraplegia.

Abby gasped. "Para..."

"There's a chance for full recovery but—he might be paralyzed from the waist down—for life."

Abby was in shock. Dr. Ingram took her hand and patted it.

"Don't worry. I'm always available for any questions you may have."

Dr. Ingram slid open the door and left.

Abby turned and looked at the unconscious Tyler. Tears streamed down her face as she hurried over to him. She sat next to his bed and gently took one of his hands and cried.

"I'll be here for you, Tyler. But I don't know if can I make it better for you this time?"

CHAPTER 6

About an hour later a strange scraping sound got her attention. At the door she saw Jeremy pulling a lounge chair into the room.

"Sorry to wake you. "Sliding the lounge chair in the corner he said, "This will make your stay more comfortable." Pointing to the chair he said, "There's a pillow and blanket on the seat there so you can stay overnight."

"Wow, I didn't expect all this. Do you do this for everybody in ICU? "

"Yeah, we try to; at least for the overnighters. Tyler's lunch tray is on my desk if you're hungry. "

Abby was starving, but she'd feel awkward eating somebody else's lunch. "Oh, that's for Tyler. I shouldn't."

"Well, look at him. It's not like he's going to eat it. He's on intravenous feeding. Besides, he's paid for it."

Oh, thank you Tyler. You're a lifesaver, even if you don't know it, yet.

Abby ate the unseasoned chicken, the dry rice and the undercooked asparagus. The roll, pudding, milk and coffee weren't half bad by comparison. She was so famished that the kitchen staff had no need to clean the plates. While the doctor and Jeremy were in the room with Tyler, Abby had time to think.

So much to do... I need to get a paper, write my next article, and find an engagement ring to keep up this charade. Getting a ring will take money, so I'll have to get to the bank. I don't have keys to my car, but Tyler's have to be around here, somewhere.

Jeremy interrupted her thoughts. "Abby, we change shifts on the hour, so if you need anything before I go you should let me know now."

"Jeremy, I have a big problem, and I think you can help."

Jeremy turned away from his computer, "Okay, what's that?"

"Well, I'm wondering what happens with Tyler's personal belongings. You see, we have two cars but the police have my keys impounded. I really need the keys to his car. "

"Oh, that. Well, his clothes are in a bag under his bed. His wallet and keys are in a safe downstairs. You can stop by on your way out."

As Abby went back into Tyler's room she looked back at Jeremy. "But, what if they don't believe me. The nurse at the front desk didn't at first. Won't you go with me to get them?"

"Sorry, but I can't. I've got to stay at my duty station. I'm sure you understand."

Abby was disappointed and very uneasy.

What if they don't believe me? What if I can't get the keys? What if I don't get his wallet? Damn, I'm sure he's got some money in it.

32

The only way to work off her frustration was to write. Abby opened her laptop and gave her full concentration to an article for the Coloradoan.

A Plumber's Nightmare

Those of you who have been in the ICU wing of a hospital know what I'm talking about. I visited my friend Tyler to see how he was recovering from the gunshot wounds he suffered during the Starbucks terrorist attack. I found him in an induced coma with tubes and wires all over his body. The Dragon space capsule couldn't have more plumbing than Tyler has on his body.

Induced coma? That was a surprise. I'm told one of the bullets impacted the spinal cord nerves, requiring surgery to remove the bullet. It'll take five days or so before we know if he's paralyzed.

Paralyzed, not dead like our news media diligently counts as they report on tragedies, and continue to tally the count each day until there are no more bodies. Yet, here I stand with a man who's not dead, as his life hangs in the balance. Lucky break and he will walk out of here. Bad luck and he'll be in a wheelchair the rest of his life. I wonder if he'll wish he were dead when he learns his plight.

I'm sorry, but did I just hear the news media talking about how many of the victims were fortunate to have non-life threatening injuries? Don't they understand that these wounded victim's lives were shattered by this event? Listen... I guess they don't. I must have been imagining things.

When Abby finished she saved the file then emailed it to Gus. Using the hospital phone she made a call.

"Gus, when you get this message, please check your e-mail. I just sent you an article I wrote about the terrorist attack.

Abby sighed as she logged off her computer.

A few minutes later a young woman showed up; a thin blond who seemed pleasant and perky. Jeremy introduced Heather to Abby, and told her that Abby would be staying 'round the clock' with Tyler.

As Jeremy prepared to leave he said to Abby, "Grab your stuff and come with me. We'll see about Tyler's things."

All Right! He is going to help me. Thank you Lord! Thank you! Thank you!

Abby packed up her laptop, and grabbed her purse. She met Jeremy in the hall and said, "OK, let's go."

"Abby," Jeremy said, "you need to be prepared for the supervisor in Admissions... Betsey."

"The receptionist mentioned her yesterday."

As they waited for the elevator Jeremy said, "She's dedicated and does a great job but putting it mildly, she can be difficult."

Abby and Jeremy stepped into the elevator. "After being in a terrorist attack, I can never imagine anything being "difficult" again."

Once on the main floor they went to the Admissions office and stood before a stern looking woman in her forties, named Betsey.

"Betsey, this is Abby. She was in the terrorist attack with one of our patients, Tyler Daly. "

Skeptical, Betsey said to Jeremy, "I hear she claims to be engaged to Mr. Daly." Betsey looked doubtfully at Abby and then down at her left hand. She folds her arms across her chest defiantly.

"I've yet to see a ring."

"I need your help, Betsey," Abby said. "I have to get my purse from the crime scene. My... my engagement ring is in my purse. All my belongings— my purse, my car, my money, my phone, and my car keys—were all cordoned off as part of the crime scene.

Betsey looked at Abby and said, "And?"

Abby continued to plead her case. "And, if I can have Ty's keys I can use his car to get my purse, return with my engagement ring and prove that Ty and I are engaged."

Jeremy intervened, saying, "Betsey, this young lady has been through a lot... the terrorist attack and Tyler's injury"

Betsey didn't soften. "Trying to play on my heartstrings, Jeremy?"

"Come on... let her have the keys."

Betsey sighed as she unfolded her arms.

"If I lose my job over this, I'll come after the both of you."

Betsey turned to the wall of file cabinets behind her. She unlocked one of the cabinets and took out Tyler's keys.

"While you're in there," Abby asked, "Can I have his wallet?

Betsey glared at Jeremy. "Now she wants his money!"

Abby pleaded, "I'm sorry Betsey, but I need the money to put gas in his car so I can go get my purse, show you my ring and keep you employed!"

Betsey handed Abby, Tyler's car keys and wallet. "After all this you better come back with a real sparkler, girl!

"Thank you so much!"

35

Jeremy smiled and told Abby, "Betsey's not as mean as she seems."

Betsey glared at Jeremy.

Causing Jeremy to say, "On second thought..."

Betsey stretched to her full 5ft. 1 in. height and slammed her fist on the counter.

"You go get that ring, girl! Right now!"

As Abby and Jeremy head off she quietly said to him, "Not sure who was worse—Betsey or the terrorists!

"I heard that!" Betsey yelled after them.

Abby and Jeremy suppress their smiles and hurried away. As they walked out of the main entrance, Abby stopped at the gift shop and bought a newspaper.

"Hey!" Jeremy said. "I thought you were anxious to get Tyler's car."

"Tyler's my focus, but I also have a job I have to keep up with. I'm a reporter for the Coloradoan."

As Abby sat on a bench just outside the door, Jeremy said, "Well, I'm impressed."

"My editor isn't, lately. That's why I wanted to get the newspaper in the gift shop so I can see if my article made it. It all seems like a million years ago, now."

"Well, gotta go. Good luck with everything." Jeremy said as he went off into the parking lot.

Abby flipped through the pages of the newspaper until she saw what she was looking for.

Here it is! A Fun Day at the Swetsville Zoo... seems pretty trivial and silly now.

Putting the newspaper aside Abby pulled out the notepad and pen she got in the gift shop, took a deep breath, and began to write.

A while later she flipped back to the first page of her notes, and began reading to herself.

Recently my best friend was badly wounded by a terrorist's bullet at a Starbucks, I was angry. I felt I had been violated. Stripped of everything—my money, credit cards, car, and phone—all impounded behind yellow crime scene tape and inaccessible for who knows how long. I still don't have them.

Then it suddenly struck me. What's wrong with this picture? I have been inconvenienced... others were killed and my friend... my best friend, was struck in the back with a terrorist's bullet. He may never walk again.

And here I was worried about my phone. I am ashamed. Lives changed forever that day in less time than it takes to order coffee at Starbucks.

CHAPTER 7

Abby sorted through Tyler's wallet to see what she could use. There was a credit card, debit card, medical card, a library card and business cards. The debit card was useless without his PIN number. But, she found $40 so she spent $10 of it on a cab to the Starbucks parking lot. She asked the driver to wait in case Tyler's car didn't start, but it did. She ran back to pay the cabbie, then scanned the area for police who might prevent her from driving away.

All clear. I'm outta' here.

As soon as Abby reached home she showered and changed into something more comfortable. Then she headed out to get things done. Her first stop was the bank to withdraw money out of her account. The bank teller smiled at her and asked, "May I see your debit card and driver's license please."

Abby was startled at the request, and responded defensively, "I'm sorry, but I lost my purse. That's why I'm here. If I had the cards you want I wouldn't need you. I could use the ATM machine."

The teller frowned and shook her head. "Sorry, no ID, no money,"

"Well, what if I can tell you my account number. Will that work?"

"I'm afraid not. Anyone could have memorized it. Why don't you come back when you have replaced your driver's license and debit card."

Abby's plan was thwarted. She was stuck with only $30 from Tyler's wallet.

At the department store she found a rather nice Cubic Zirconium ring for $28.00, and the clerk was able to squeeze the band small enough to fit her finger. When she prepared to check out Abby nervously withdrew Tyler's credit card to pay. Nothing was said, which surprised her. She expected to be questioned.

"Here you go miss, just sign here, please," requested the clerk.

Abby calmly signed as Mrs. Tyler Daly and handed the receipt to the clerk. "Here you go. Thanks for your help."

As Abby folded her receipt she couldn't help but reflect on her signature.

Mrs. Tyler Daly. Isn't it odd that as soon as Tyler says he wants to marry me, I'm signing a document as if I'm his wife? Is this an omen?

Heading straight for the door, Abby felt like a thief. Walking quickly, she just knew someone was following her. Not wanting to look over her shoulder, she made it out of the store, and hustled to her car, checking the reflection in each store window looking for some security guard trying to catch her. She wasn't comfortable until she drove out of the parking lot. Then she heaved a big sigh of relief. Using the credit card worked better than she imagined.

Maybe she could use Tyler's credit card for other things until she got her purse back.

Entering the hospital, Abby proudly held up her left hand as she approached the information center to show off the engagement ring.

"Very well," the attendant said. "I'm glad you found it."

Heather, the ICU nurse was still on duty when Abby arrived at Tyler's room.

"Hi Heather. How is he?"

"Hi Abby. There's no change. Don't expect any for a few days."

Abby plopped down in the lounge chair and stared at Tyler as she listened to the monitor's pulsating throbs and pings. She felt so sad seeing him like this. He was looking worse every day. His hair was matted and he needed a shave. Holding his hand as she looked over the medical apparatus and into his eyes. "Tyler," she whispered. "Please wake up and walk."

CHAPTER 8

Abby was quiet, watching Tyler with some expectation he had heard her and would soon respond accordingly when Jeremy walked in and said, "Abby, you'll have to leave the room for a few minutes so we can move Tyler. He will be gone for a while in order to run tests on him."

"Tests? What kind of tests?"

"The usual MRI's, PET Scans, ultrasounds. Doc wants them to evaluate his level of mobility."

"When will we know the results?"

"Can't say. It'll take at least a day, maybe two. Why don't you go home and get some real rest. This is going to take a few hours."

Abby was weary as she climbed the stairs to her apartment. Suddenly, she was alarmed when she sensed someone was right behind her. Quickly, she turned around to see the smiling face of a police officer.

He politely asked, "Would you know a Miss Abigail Porter who lives in this building?"

"Yes, I'm Abby Porter. Did something bad happen?"

"I don't think getting your purse back is bad. Do you?"

"Oh, bless you. I have my life back. Or, at least part of it."

"Before I can release this purse to you, I'll need to see some ID, ma'am."

"My picture ID is in the purse." Abby began to reach her hand into the purse, and then paused. "May I?"

The officer nodded his approval.

Abby retrieved her wallet and showed the police officer her driver's license and photograph. "Will this do?" She asked.

"It sure will," the officer answered. "Glad we could return it to you." He tipped his hat and walked away.

Abby climbed the stairs to her apartment grateful to have her keys. She and plopped on the couch and let out a deep sigh.

Finally, I feel whole again.

***

Two days after Tyler's tests, Dr. Ingram quietly entered Tyler's room, surprising Abby.

"Abby, I'm glad you're here. Will you please come with me so we can talk in private?"

The doctor's request made Abby uncomfortable, although she said "Sure," as she got up out of her chair. She hesitated, and asked, "What's going on?"

Dr. Ingram placed his hand on her shoulder as they started down the hallway together. "We need to talk about Tyler's test results."

Abby had a bad feeling about going to his office, even though the doctor was soft spoken and kind. His request seemed far too formal, and reminded her of stories she'd heard when patients are advised they have cancer. Now she was the nervous one.

The doctor motioned to a chair, "Please have a seat."

Abby sat, fidgeting. She crossed her legs one way, then the other, never getting comfortable. She hoped Dr. Ingram was going to talk about moving Tyler out of intensive care, but couldn't be sure.

The doctor rested his arms on his desk before speaking. "Abby, I've looked at Tyler's test results. Tyler has improved a lot since the surgery. His condition has not worsened. However, there is a serious side to his injury that we can't mitigate."

"He's paralyzed, just like you said. Isn't he?"

"Yes Abby, Tyler is paralyzed."

Abby jumped out of her chair and threw her arms in an outburst. "Damned terrorists can kill and maim, then just walk away leaving people like Tyler behind to suffer for it." She paced across the doctor's office.

"Abby," the doctor said.

She turned toward Dr. Ingram.

"Please be seated, Abby. Hear me out."

"I can't sit." Abby's hands were shaking. She leaned against the office door as her mind raced through all the implications of Tyler being paralyzed.

"Abby, the bullet impacted the nerves in the thoracic area of the spine. Called T7 to be exact. I was hoping the nerves would recover when I removed the pressure of the bullet, but they didn't. The nerves aren't any worse after the surgery, mind you, but the damage has caused paraplegia."

Abby finally slumped into a chair, with her head down and staring at her hands. She had no idea what to say.

Dr. Ingram continued, but spoke softly. "So, there's little I can do now except to reduce the sedatives so I can move Tyler out of ICU. Probably two days. Then I'll release him to a rehabilitation facility where he can begin therapy to adjust to his condition."

Abby continued to sit in silence.

"Are you going to be okay, Abby?"

She took a deep breath, raised her head to look at the doctor and said, "No. I don't think I'll ever be okay. And neither will Tyler. He's lost his new job at the University of Texas. He won't be able to volunteer at the children's home any more. Everything he treasures will be gone."

"I'm terribly sorry. I understand you are very close friends. Do you wish to tell Tyler yourself, or would you prefer that I do?"

Abby looked up quickly. "Oh, there's no way I can tell him."

"I'm sorry it has to be this way. I'll explain it to Tyler. Another thing Abby, are you familiar with the Craig Hospital in Denver."

Thinking was a distraction at the moment, but she said, "I may have heard of it, but I can't remember now."

"Abby, Tyler's best chance to recover his mobility is at the Craig Hospital. Anything less and you might as well tie him to a wheelchair for life."

Abby slumped in her chair. "Dr. Ingram, I have a hard time believing he'll be paralyzed for life. What about all the research going on? Shouldn't paraplegia be the first to be cured."

"I would certainly hope so, Abby. But it's not going to be this year, or the next. And, Tyler must learn to live with the present, in spite of your hopes that his disability will go away."

Since there was little more she could say, Abby stood up, thanked Dr. Ingram and left his office. She was shocked and saddened by the news. Walking the halls back to Tyler's room Abby was in a daze, barely noticing housekeepers, nurses, or the nursing stations she passed by. And her nervous tension only got worse knowing any day Tyler would wake up and learn the awful news.

CHAPTER 9

In no mood to talk to anybody Abby began to shut off her phone ringing when she saw it was her editor.

Oh, I want to shut out the world so badly.

She chose to answer the call. "What's up Gus?"

"Abby, we need more from you about this guy who was shot at Starbucks."

"Gus, it's not 'this guy'." He has a name and it's Tyler Daly. And, I don't know what more I can say about it."

"Well, you're in the hospital with him aren't you? What's that like? What's happening?

"Gus, I'm completely out of ammunition to share. Don't you understand?"

"Listen, the public is eating this up. It's a hot story. I'll double your pay for each article you send me, but only if I get one for tomorrow's run."

Double? Something's going on that I don't know about. How did this story become so important?

"Okay, Gus. I'll have something ready by midnight. Now, can I go?"

"Perfect. I know you can do it."

This time Abby did shut off her phone. Once back in Tyler's room she opened her laptop and typed out her next article.

Worse Than Dying

What on earth could be worse than dying? Well, we'll find out when my friend Tyler comes out of his medically induced coma.

You see, that's when he'll learn that all his dreams are broken, and life as he knows it will never be the same again.

The bullet wound in his back has caused paralysis from the waist down, and I know he'll think the curse of paralysis is worse than dying. Truthfully, I can't say that I wouldn't feel the same.

Abby looked out the hospital window into the dark night.

Gus will like this, but will Tyler?

Close to midnight Tyler started mumbling incoherently just as Abby was forwarding her article to the newspaper. She stepped out of the room to notify Jeremy, and then quickly returned to Tyler's bedside.

Feeling his hand move in hers was thrilling. His eyes were even open. "Tyler, it's so wonderful that you're awake now."

"If I'm awake why do I feel like I'm in the fog?"

"Well, you've been asleep for 10 days now, waiting for your wounds to heal. Take your time, there's no hurry."

"Am I more beautiful after sleeping so long?"

Tears filled Abby's eyes. "You're beautiful to me. You could have died in that attack, Tyler. Letting her emotions lead her, she was hugging him when Dr. Ingram entered the room.

Dr. Ingram sat beside Tyler's bed. "Glad to see you up and awake. How are you feeling, my friend?"

"I feel like I just came out of hibernation. Abby said I've been in a coma. My legs are awfully numb."

"Your incision has healed well. However, the nerves have not healed."

Tyler lay back on his pillow, commenting, "I assume the nerves heal last?"

"Tyler," Dr. Ingram said, "they aren't going to heal."

Immediately Tyler looked at Abby, whose face was drawn with tears on her cheeks. He looked back at Dr. Ingram.

"What are you saying?"

"Tyler, the bullet went into your back above the lumbar area, about belly button high. It nicked the thoracic T7 vertebra. So, I performed surgery immediately to remove the bullet and relieve the pressure on your nerves. It's the best chance we had for the nerves to heal."

"So why the coma?"

"It was a precaution. I didn't want you moving around during the recovery process."

"Fine, now that I'm awake, Doc, what's it gonna take to get outta' here?"

"That's the easy part, Tyler. I'll start the orders now, and you can be discharged just as soon as arrangements are made for your therapy and rehab. We'll also have to schedule an airlift for you to Craig Hospital in Englewood."

Puzzled at the doctor's words, Tyler looked at Abby first, then the doctor. "Why can't I just walk out of here when the numbness in my legs goes away?"

"I'm sorry to say the surgical procedure didn't correct the damage, Tyler. Your nerves didn't recover, and you've lost muscle control and sensation from your hips down. It's what we call paraplegia. But in time, it's my belief that you'll begin to feel a little bit of sensation in your lower extremities."

Tyler became agitated and tried to sit up to face the doctor, but failed. In frustration and anger he addressed the doctor. "You're saying I'm paralyzed, aren't you?"

"I'm afraid so. But Tyler, you're young and strong enough to deal with this change in your life. It won't be easy. The road to live with immobility is very difficult. That's why I want you to go to the Craig Hospital in Denver. It's your best chance to recover as much of your mobility as possible."

Abby had been quietly watching Tyler's reaction throughout the conversation and decided that if Tyler had to be confined to a wheelchair, the least she could do is stay by his side and help him adjust. After all, he was prepared to make a commitment to her when they met at Starbucks. She needed to support him, too.

As Dr. Ingram left the room Abby moved to the bed, held his hand and put her head on his shoulder. "I'm so sorry, Tyler. So sorry! You know I'd take your place just so you could walk again."

"I know you would." Patting her shoulder he said, "Don't take this so hard. I'm the one who just got a life sentence."

"Oh, quit it," she said poking him in the ribs, "What a way to talk!"

"How'd you get time off work to be here, anyway?" Tyler asked.

"I've been writing from here, as if it's any of your business. Lots of writers work from remote locations. Why can't I? Besides, you're going to need help, and who's going to do that for you, huh?"

"I can manage. I have before."

"Come on Tyler, you aren't going to just get up and walk home, are you? You can't drive yourself to therapy for the next two to three months, can you? Someone will have to cook your meals until you figure out how. There's laundry, and ironing. You know, "housekeeper" stuff. Get real! You're the one who proposed marriage. Isn't this what a wife would do for her husband?

"Forget about that. As I recall I was a whole man with a future then. Now, I'm half a man without a job. I won't have you giving up your career to live my paralyzed life."

Abby's eyes glared at Tyler. "Oh, you won't will you? Well, I'm glad I never answered your proposal because I could never live with a man who thought he could tell me what to do!"

"You're not understanding me," he said forcefully. "I can't ask you to live my life, and push me around in a wheelchair. I want you to pursue your own dreams. Be successful. Get married and have children. You have to understand this is very important to me, Abby. You have a wonderful life ahead of you, and I have a totally different one ahead of me. I refuse to drag you into it."

Abby got up and started to leave his room. Stopping at the door she looked back at him. "Tyler Daly, you're an insensitive, self-centered jerk. Why do I even bother?"

53

CHAPTER 10

Abby stood beside Dr. Ingram on the hospital roof, watching attendants load Tyler onto the Medevac helicopter. The flight would take him to Craig Hospital in the Denver suburb of Englewood. Abby was not allowed on the flight, and would have to drive there alone.

About two hours later Abby entered the parking lot of Craig Hospital. It didn't look like the hospital she imagined. It was a one-story building with a brilliant white exterior, and walls of glass shining like jewels. There was a dome over the lobby that gave her the impression it housed a telescope.

This doesn't look like any hospital I'm used to seeing.

She pulled into a circular drive that looked like a typical hotel entrance, and stopped when an aide came out to meet her.

"Who are you here to see, ma'am?" he asked.

"Tyler Daly. He arrived by Medevac this morning."

"Yes, Mrs. Daly, we've been expecting you," the aide said as he pointed toward the parking lot. "You can park in that visitors row for today. You'll get an assigned spot by tomorrow, okay?"

This is the second time I've been called Mrs. Daly. Is this some joke, or just practice?

Abby parked her car and walked into the hospital lobby.

"Hello. Ms. Abby Porter I presume?"

"I am," Abby replied, "but I just got here. How would you know me?"

"Tyler's description of you was spot on. Well, actually you're more attractive than he said you were."

"Really? He's never told me I was attractive?"

"Forgive me, I must introduce myself. I'm Kenny Hosack, the Director of Public Relations for Craig Hospital. Tyler and his Interdisciplinary Team are just beginning their meeting. We'd like you to join him, so please follow me."

A Team? What's that about?

She followed Mr. Hosack into a very large conference room. However, it didn't seem so large when the space was taken up by 18 people... some in white coats, some in workout clothes, and others in street clothes. Everyone was very pleasant, and they each greeted Abby as she joined Tyler at the head of the long, polished slate table.

"Mr. Daly," Kenny Hosack asked, "May we call you Tyler?"

Tyler seemed overwhelmed by the size of the group in front of him, and just nodded.

"Very well then. Ladies and gentlemen, I'll leave Tyler in your charge. Patting him on the shoulder, Mr. Hosack said, "Nice to meet you."

Still overwhelmed, Tyler simply said, "Yes, me too."

If Tyler thought the size of the group was overwhelming, it was nothing compared to the jobs and titles of people as they

56

introduced themselves. Dr. Koplan was head of the Team, which included doctors, nurses, and therapists. The doctors and nurses covered cardiac and respiratory treatment, and well as nerve pain management. When the physical therapists were introduced they talked about their positions in physical, occupational, music, speech therapy or adaptive driving. There was a psychologist for mental health support, a chaplain for spiritual support, a dietician and a pharmacist.

Tyler should have felt like a king, surrounded by such a group of specialists. Instead it scared the hell out of him. If it took this many people to care for him, his paralysis must be much worse than he thought.

Dr. Koplan addressed Abby, "Abby, let me begin by saying that we traditionally ask spouses to be a part of the patient's care."

Abby stood quickly, saying, "Excuse me, but we are not married. Tyler and I have been friends since childhood and I'm just here as... as she waved her hand she noticed the engagement ring was still on her finger and immediately had to change course... I mean that I'm here as Tyler's fiancée. My name is Abby Porter."

She could feel Tyler's eyes on her, the moment she said "fiancée."

"I see," Dr. Koplan said. "Well, I don't think that will make any difference. You see, Abby, we have apartments on campus for family members so they can be near their loved ones and assist them in their therapy sessions. As a bride to be, you and Tyler qualify and will be assigned an apartment while Tyler's in rehab. If that's alright with you?"

Will that be alright with me? Of course! I've been thinking so much about Tyler I haven't spent a minute thinking about where I'll live. Thank you, you cheap little ring. You're so handy.

Addressing the doctor she said, "Yes, thank you so much. But you mentioned participating and assisting in therapy sessions. I wasn't expecting that. What could I possibly do for Tyler?"

"Family support is a crucial part of Tyler's recovery. First of all he'll need your constant encouragement. Second, you'll need to understand what he's going through and learning about his healing in order to continue supporting him beyond his time here. We want you to be part of Tyler's Team, meaning you're invited to all of our Team meetings and therapy sessions... especially the daily clinics covering his routine skin care, sexuality and bladder and bowel elimination procedures.

When the introductions were over, and other members of the Team left the room, Dr. Koplan introduced Tyler's pain therapist, Dr. Jill Hoover. Dr. Koplan then left and Dr. Hoover sat in a chair beside Tyler.

"Tyler," she said, "There's something we need to cover right away. Have you been experiencing what we call 'nerve' pain?"

"I'm not sure what that means, exactly," Tyler said, "but I have some burning sensations in my hips."

"That's an example of nerve pain, Tyler. You may also feel sharp, stabbing, or tingling sensations, from time to time, that are more intense. I've written this prescription for a medication to help reduce the nerve pain you have that will probably get worse as your rehab gets more intense. But, we'll monitor that closely."

"Really?"

"Yes, so please don't stop taking this prescription just because you feel good. Experience tells me that we'll probably have to increase the dosage sometime during your rehab."

"Ok, I'll remember that."

"This second prescription is an anti-depressant. You may feel good now and think you don't need it, but your emotions will jump around like a kid at a parade. You'll have denial, anger, and times when you're scared to death. Trust me, I've seen it all and no one is exempt.

"Does feeling overwhelmed count?" Tyler asked.

Dr. Hoover smiled, saying, "Yes, it does. That's natural on your first day, but it usually goes away the first week here. I want you to take these two prescriptions daily. We may have to add some others later, but we'll decide when the time comes. Okay, I think Roger's waiting for you outside. He'll take you over to our financial services department."

"Thank you, doctor," Tyler said as Abby pushed him out of the room, to join Roger Alter, his rehabilitation coordinator.

Roger appeared to be in his early fifty's but he wasn't built like it. He was solid. Slim waist, broad shoulders and chest with arms that didn't have that aging sag. They were stout.

"Hi Abby," Roger said, "You and I will be working together. And Tyler, by the time you're through rehab, you'll be independent, mobile, and able to drive a car. I expect you'll be an expert gymnast and accomplished swimmer... and you'll be playing basketball and even be skiing by first snow.

Tyler thought Roger was crazy. "I couldn't do a lot of those things when I could walk. I know everyone means well but right now, I can't envision any of it—and I certainly can't envision ever getting used to all this as a new way of living."

Abby kept an eye on Tyler who appeared to be somewhere between anger and misery. She continued rolling him down the hallway in his wheelchair as Roger showed them around. Roger pointed to a closed double door.

"That's the gym and beyond that is the swimming pool, Tyler. Tomorrow will be your first full day of therapy.

Unenthusiastically, Tyler said, "Thanks for the warning."

A short distance further Roger gestured towards a door with a sign that reads, "Pain Therapy."

"This is Dr. Hoover's office," Roger said.

Tyler stared at Roger, slightly puzzled.

"Tyler," Roger said, "everyone who experiences the trauma you did goes through the same stages of grief as we do when losing a loved one."

Tyler agreed. "That makes sense. I lost a loved one—me—the man I used to be."

CHAPTER 11

Roger was taking Tyler to his next appointment. "The Financial Office is just down the hall. You'll need to stop by there," he said.

Tyler bowed his head as he said, "And get more depressed, right?"

Roger chuckled.

"Actually, it shouldn't be that bad," Tyler said in a more upbeat tone. "I have medical insurance with a $2 million cap."

"Yes," Abby said, "I brought a copy of his policy."

Roger looked wary. "Well, you can talk to Mary in Finance. She'll go over everything.

As they went into her office Mary Davis, a middle-aged woman, greeted them.

Abby immediately noticed a picture of a little boy in a frame on Mary 's desk. "Oh, what a handsome little boy," she said.

"This is my very first grandchild. I'm so proud of him!"

"You should be," Abby replied, "What's his name?"

"Don, he's only two years old in that picture, but is he ever a handful. Quite an adventurer already! Well, since I'm responsible for managing your fees and payments during rehabilitation, we'd better get started."

After reviewing the charges for Tyler and Abby's expected two months of rehabilitation and their assigned apartment, Mary opened the discussion about insurance coverage.

"This part should be easy," Tyler said, "I've got a two million dollar policy. We certainly won't spend that much on rehab, will we?"

"Oh, Mr. Daly, we will not. However, there might be one little misunderstanding."

Tyler frowned. "What kind of misunderstanding?"

"From what I see here in your insurance policy it is two million dollars, as you said, but that's the cap on the policy. They won't pay more than two million. However, the amount the policy pays out is a maximum of $20,000 per year."

Tyler's reaction was to slam his fists into the wheelchair arms. "What! They said two million dollars when I bought it!"

"Unfortunately, this happens often. What I was going to say is that your initial ICU care was covered by your health insurance, but you're still left with a large co-pay for the full ten weeks. The $55,000 Medevac flight from Ft. Collins was not covered by your insurance either."

Frustrated, Tyler looked at Abby, and then Mary, "What can I do now? Check out?"

Abby put her hand on his arm and said, "Tyler, don't get upset. We'll find a way out of this. You're going nowhere. It'll be alright."

Mary added, "Please keep me informed of your progress. I am obliged to tell you that you must have a financial plan in place in order to remain at Craig.

Tyler sighed and looked at Abby. Abby tried to give him encouragement. "I'll check out some loans at my bank. We'll figure it out."

Because Tyler averted her eyes, Mary looked over and offered a smile of encouragement to Abby.

Disturbed by the lack of finances, Tyler and Abby joined Roger again, who took them to the lobby. "Okay, now, here's the reception desk." Turning to the receptionist Roger said, "Vickie, this is Tyler Daly and Abby Porter. Will you have someone show them to their apartment?"

"Of course, Roger."

"If you folks can wait in the lobby for a moment," Vickie said, pointing to some lounge chairs, "I'll get someone from PR to come up here and help you."

"Abby," Roger said, "the apartments are furnished, so you won't need much to get settled. Will I see you with Tyler tomorrow?"

Abby look up, "Actually, I wasn't expecting this type of commitment, Roger. I'm working remotely for the Coloradoan in Ft. Collings. I want to be here while he is evaluated, for sure. There's a lot of work for me to do to help him adjust and find financing for his care."

"Would they give you a leave of absence?" Roger asked.

Abby shrugged. "I think it's my only choice. I'll call and request a leave today."

"Wonderful. We'll see you tomorrow at Tyler's eight o'clock Team meeting then. Have a good evening."

As they sat in the lobby, waiting, Abby said to Tyler, "This is not what I was expecting. This place is extremely intense, and they expect a serious commitment from me. I'm not sure I can do it."

"Me either," Tyler remarked. Rubbing his numb legs he said, "A bullet wound and I can't feel my legs. Now they want to assign all these people to help me. It's ridiculous. Just get me up and help me walk. That's all I want. I don't need a 'Team'."

"I agree. It's a whole new world. How do we handle it?"

There was no time to answer, as they were interrupted.

"Hello, pardon my interruption. I'm Carol Wainwright, the housing coordinator. Please follow me to our apartment complex."

Out the front door of the hospital they turned left. At the end of the sidewalk Abby pushed Tyler's now familiar wheelchair across a service road, then another forty yards to an apartment module on the left. The alcove provided protective covering for two facing doors, one for each apartment.

"Here you go, folks, Unit 11 on the left here is fully furnished from kitchen to bathroom. It'll be a little unusual for you, Abby, because it's a handicapped unit. You will find the counters are lower and tables are lower, too. You know, accommodations for a wheelchair bound person."

The two-bedroom apartment was very nice, a bit outdated but clean. The first thing Tyler noticed was the lack of doors. A partial wall in the center of the room separated the kitchen from the living room. A u-shaped sectional fit against the partial wall, with end tables and lamps on the ends, but no coffee table in the center to block wheelchair access. Open passages on either end of the wall were about six feet wide. There was no dining room or kitchenette. Instead the room had a breakfast bar, which could be lowered to accommodate the handicapped in wheelchairs.

Tyler looked pleased. "Pretty cool, huh, Abby?"

"Yes, it's very nice."

Ms. Wainwright gave each a key, wished them a wonderful stay, and, left them on their own.

Tyler and Abby explored the apartment. Abby was able to adjust the kitchen counter to make it lower.

"You don't have to lower it. I'm not cooking," Tyler said.

Abby looked at him over her shoulder. "That would be a job for your wife, I take it."

"I don't have a wife."

Investigating the kitchen cabinets Abby said, "You still haven't allowed me to answer your proposal. You didn't know that we are engaged... sort of."

Abby rolled Tyler into the living room through the wide archways. "You notice how all the doorways are wide and have no doors."

Tyler nodded, "Yeah, that's for us disabled."

Abby sighed and plopped down on the couch.

Tyler rolled close to the couch. "What's this about us being engaged?"

"They wouldn't let me in to see you unless I was family. I convinced them that I was your fiancée, which I almost was.

"Almost is the key word."

Abby smiled at Tyler. "You told me you loved me, Tyler before..."

"Yeah," Tyler said. "Before is the key word."

Abby folded her hands and leaned onto her knees. "Your feelings haven't changed, have they?"

Tyler backed away a bit. "No, but... obviously everything else has. I mean you're still my best friend but... it's just not something I want to talk about now."

"Okay... anytime you're ready I'm here. And any time you want my answer, I'm also ready with that."

Tyler looked stern when he said, "Let me remind you that I withdrew the proposal."

"I'm not sure you can legally do that." Abby laughed, making Tyler crack a smile.

It was a good time to change the subject, so Tyler said, "Hey, since we're almost engaged are we sharing the same bedroom?"

Shaking her head, Abby said, "Oh, so now, when it comes to bedtime, we're almost engaged! This is a two-bedroom unit, my man. One bedroom is for you—and one is for your best friend!"

Abby leaned down, kissed Tyler on the forehead and headed off to the bedroom.

"I'm exhausted and heading to the "best friend" suite right now."

As Tyler watched her he smiled and shook his head.

The next morning when Tyler rolled into the kitchen Abby was eating a bowl of cereal. He moved up next to her so he could look into her eyes and asked, "Are you mad at me?"

"No." She said.

"Good. I'd hoped you'd still love me. You know we need to be at the hospital in thirty minutes don't you? I'm going to need your help getting dressed, too."

"Of course."

CHAPTER 12

The day was full of firsts. It was Tyler's first day of therapy and the first time they had to deal with his wheelchair. Needing to drive downtown Denver for a meeting, Abby planned to shuttle Tyler to the hospital on her way.

Pushing Tyler to the car Abby asked, "You don't seem excited to start therapy, Tyler. Is everything all right?"

"I really don't see why I have to do this, Abby. After all, I'm in a chair now, and I'll be in a chair when this is over. So, what's the point?"

"That's a pretty defeatist attitude, don't you think? What if all this helps you to walk again? Ever think of it that way?"

"I don't think it's possible, Abby."

"Well, you should. Here's my car. Can you get in it alright?"

"Yea, just hold the wheelchair steady and I'll use the door for support."

Tyler swung his butt onto the seat of the two-door Toyota Corolla. It almost broke Abby's heart to watch Tyler pick up each leg with his hands and place it inside the car.

"Can I close the door now?" She asked.

"Yeah, I'm okay."

Rolling the wheelchair around to the driver's side, Abby moved the seat forward so there was room to slide the collapsed chair into the back seat. It was awkward.

"How in the world am I going to get this in the car?"

Tyler turned to look behind the driver's seat. "Can you put it in with the large wheels first, then roll it toward to passenger side?"

Abby grunted as she pulled the chair out of the car to start over. Putting the wheels first she pushed and shoved. It stuck on Tyler's seat.

"Do you think you could pull your seat all the way forward so I have some more room?"

"Sure." Tyler moved the seat forward and leaned forward. "Ohhh! Man, this is hurting my legs."

Abby stopped and glared at Tyler. "One more wise crack like that and you can roll this damn chair to the hospital yourself. Capish?"

"Yeah, yeah! Have you got enough room now?"

Abby reached in and rolled a wheel with her hand and the chair moved across the floor and rested against the opposite door.

"Whew!" Abby got in the driver's seat and started the car. "Is it going to be this difficult every time?"

Tyler smirked, just a little. "No it won't. Actually that chair breaks down into four parts to make it easy to load."

Abby's earring almost came off when she snapped her head toward Tyler. "You let me struggle with that damn thing when we could have taken it apart?"

"I don't know how to do it yet. It's something I'm supposed to learn at Craig's."

"Well, let me tell you something, Daly, if you ever want to ride with me again, that better be the first thing you learn!"

When they arrived at the hospital Tyler turned his head away and remained silent as Abby struggled to remove his wheelchair from her small car. It didn't come out much easier than it went in. He opened the door and she pushed the chair close by so he could grab the handles and move into the chair.

When Abby pushed Tyler into the lobby the receptionist met them warmly, and Abby left Tyler to wait for his physical therapist. Looking around Tyler watched people come and go with purpose. It seemed like a very active place.

I wonder what's going to happen to me today.

Roger appeared momentarily, asking, "Well, Tyler, how is your apartment? Comfortable enough?"

"It's very nice," Tyler said. "Thank you."

"Good. This morning I'm going to give you a tour of our facilities, and then we'll review your program. After lunch the action begins. We've got things to do today, so we'd better move along. Follow me."

The first group of patients Roger showed him was engaged in learning wheelchair skills. "Here's where you will get familiar with your chair and its capabilities. These people are learning how to break it down and reassemble it. Later on, in wheel chair class we teach endurance, curbs and stair negotiations.

"They can do all that?" Abby asked Roger.

"Oh, yes, everyone does. Come along now, this is the fitness class. Here we emphasize upper body strength. Eventually, if you're capable, we have outdoor hand-cycling and wheelchair sports like basketball and even sit skiing."

Tyler shook his head. "Really? People like me can do those things? I've never been athletic. I'm more of an artist."

Roger asked Tyler, "Oh, do you paint?"

"I sketch sometimes, but basically I'm a pianist."

"Well, how interesting. We don't get many pianists here. Lily, your music therapist, will be pleased to hear this. We have a piano in the lobby that you can play in your free time. Now, come on down here to the mat class."

Watching people dragging their bodies from the floor onto chairs and couches seemed odd to Tyler.

Why don't they just get up and sit in them?

The reality of the thought startled Tyler. Here he was in a wheel chair and his mind was still in the normal world!

"Are you okay, Tyler?" Roger asked as he placed his hand on his shoulder.

"Sorry," Tyler said, shaking his head as if to clear out cobwebs, "I just had a flashback. Really weird."

"Yeah, that happens to everybody now and then. It usually goes away on its own, though. We'll finish up here at the pool, where you'll work on strength, endurance and range of motion."

Looking toward the pool Tyler suddenly felt overwhelmed. "Roger, I can't swim."

Leaning on the railing Roger looked at Tyler. "That's alright. You'll grow into it. You'll be surprised what you'll be able to do after two months here. You'll start slowly and work your way through all of these activities. It will be challenging, that's for sure. That's why you'll need Abby's encouragement."

Roger stopped at a set of double doors. "Oh, here's the cafeteria. Let's have lunch."

When were seated at a table with their lunch trays, Roger explained what Tyler could expect.

"Eventually patients grow strong and challenge the process to speed up their recovery. In a relatively short period they regain ability as we nurture their independence. Many find an outlet, be it swimming, basketball, wheelchair racing or snow skiing."

Tyler couldn't believe what he was hearing

"Well," Roger said, "you'll try them all. The biggest thrill I see is when a patient goes skiing. Everyone who tries it just loves the rush of movement and wind in the face experience."

CHAPTER 13

After lunch Roger took Tyler to the mats for stretching. And it wasn't your yoga type stretching. He started pulling Tyler's legs up toward his shoulders. First lifting just one leg at a time, and then two at a time. Later he pulled Tyler's arms over his head and across his chest. Finally, Roger rolled him onto his stomach and helped him find his ankles to pull up onto his stomach in a boat shape.

Tyler interrupted their routine. "I'm beat, Roger, how much more do you have planned?"

"Your stamina will improve. I was trying to break down the muscle atrophy and tendon contracture in your ankles, knees and hips. And in case you haven't caught on yet, you'll depend on your upper body the rest of your life."

"I got that part already."

"Look around, you'll see both men and women with tight, trim upper bodies. Without a strong upper body you're just a snail draggin' yourself around. So, let's call it a day. Get some rest. The next day or two you'll be going through our evaluation process and a CT scan of your injury."

"Roger, this is too much! I'm paralyzed for God's sake! What's there to evaluate?"

"Tyler, your evaluation will allow us to categorize the degree of your motor and sensory impairment."

"Which is that I can't walk, and I have no feeling in my legs." Tyler remarked.

"Technically speaking, Tyler, we will use pinprick and light touch techniques to assess twenty-eight areas of the skin supplied by nerves from a single spinal root, and ten key muscles. Your sensory and motor readings become A.I.S.A scores. Pronounced like 'Asia,' they determine your therapy program and your chances of walking out of here."

"So, what does Asia mean Roger?"

"A.I S.A. means the American Spinal Injury Association. The scores are the essential minimal elements of neurologic assessment for patients with spinal cord injuries. We just use the term AISA around here."

Tyler nodded. "If you say so, Roger. I don't see much hope in it."

"Okay, here's the pharmacy. He's all yours Maria."

"Thank you Roger. You're Tyler Daly, right?" she asked.

"That's me."

Maria placed two bottles of tablets on the counter. "These are ready for you. All that's left is for you to take 'em."

Tyler gave Maria a weak smile while placing the containers in his pocket.

Why would I want to take these if they aren't going to help me walk?

***

Abby desperately needed a night out with her friends in Denver. They agreed to meet at the Sport's Page, a three story warehouse converted into a bar and music venue. The place was huge, with a full bar at both sides of the first floor, the second floor and even the third floor. From the third floor a suspended glass DJ's room could be seen hanging over the massive dance floor in the center of the building. Tonight a five-piece country western band was playing.

"How's Tyler doing at the hospital, Abby?" Her friend Aleese asked. She was Abby's closest friend... like a sister. A tall brunette with a sweet attractive smile, her square shoulders and slightly heavy legs made her appear intimidating. First meeting at Colorado State University they had shared a dorm room for three years.

"How is who?" Abby said.

"Tyler! How is Tyler?" Aleese repeated."

Abby could see that Aleese was talking to her, but she could hardly hear a word. The lights were flashing on the stage of the Sports Page where the band was playing so loud the whole place throbbed like a pulse. The crowd of almost 1000 was crushing together making it impossible to move about. Abby was forced to hold her drink up to her chest so she wouldn't spill it.

"Sue," Abby yelled, "can you hear what Aleese is saying?"

Sue was a sweetie. Only five-feet-two inches tall, she had a nice build above the waist, but her wide hips and thick legs didn't seem to fit her body, which attracted attention but not by many men.

"No," Sue said. "Let's move away from here so we can talk." Sue waved to Aleese to follow them.

Just as Abby turned away from the band she was shoved in the back, spilling her fresh glass of wine down her chest. She turned fiercely on the culprit, and faced a middle aged blond man about six feet two, acting like nothing had happened.

"Look at what you did!" She shouted at him. "This is a new blouse, you idiot! Where'd you learn to walk? Don't you have any manners? Here," she said as she threw the remaining wine into his face, "why don't you finish it?"

Shocked, the man spoke as he wiped wine from his face, "I'm terribly sorry if I'm responsible. Please, let me..."

There was no one left to listen as Abby and her friends rushed towards the ladies' room.

"Excuse me sir," said a waiter carrying drinks. "You can use my towel if you wish."

"Thank you very much. Could you please refresh my drink? I'm quite finished with hers."

In the rest room the three women worked quickly to dry off Abby and rinse the wine out of her blouse. Then they agreed they should take Abby home.

When she turned the handle on the apartment door, it didn't move...it was locked. Her immediate worry was for Tyler, who never leaves the door locked if he is home.

Did he leave the apartment alone? How could he? It's so risky.

Taking the key from her purse she unlocked the door and cautiously entered the apartment only to see Tyler near the couch reading the newspaper. Relieved, Abby closed the door and set her purse down.

"Tyler, why is the door locked?"

"It's a special effort to keep my friends in and reporters out."

"Do you mean me? I'm your friend...and I'm also a newspaper reporter."

"Exactly. One of you isn't welcome."

Abby was hurt, and deeply suspicious. She hadn't seen Tyler behave this way in a very long time. Quickly scanning around the room, it looked like he'd been reading the paper for a while, the way sections were spread on the couch and floor. "So, I take it you read my article."

"Yep," he said still hiding behind the paper.

"So, what did you think of it?"

"I thought a self-centered reporter used a friend's weaknesses to enhance her reputation."

Abby had walked to the sectional and stood with her hands on her hips and eyes trying to burrow a hole in Tyler's newspaper so he could see her displeasure. "You can't be serious! I would never do that."

Tyler dropped the paper to his lap, and gave Abby an icy look. "Too late. You already did."

"Well, just what is this reporter supposed to do? Forget the story and leave everyone in the dark about why, what, and how paraplegics recover from traumatic injury?"

"I'm not telling you what to do. I'm telling you to leave me out of it, or I'll make a public statement that you're pregnant with my baby."

Abby's hand covered her mouth, gasping as Tyler's incredulous threat startled her. "Tyler Daly, you wouldn't dare do that! I know you. You're not mean."

"You name me in one more of your articles and you'll have a chance to find out, won't you? I don't want to see my name in print again. If I do, so will you. An eye for an eye."

Tyler has never behaved this way with me. He usually has an thread of humor in a conversation, and there isn't one. Have I been so unprofessional with my closest friend, when I should have asked his permission?

CHAPTER 14

Tyler asked Roger, "T7—ASIA C, incomplete? What does that mean?" "Two days of tests and that's it? T7-ASIA C? It sounds like a seat assignment on a flight to China."

"Oh, but it's much more important. It's hope, Tyler. T7 is the location of the vertebrae, just about belly button level. ASIA is the Asia Spinal Injury Associations rating scale. And C, incomplete, means there's not total and permanent nerve damage. With hard work, time and dedication you could walk again."

Abby reached over and ruffled Tyler's hair, "Isn't that good news?"

"It's just another way of saying I'm paralyzed," he said, "I think I'd prefer the flight to China."

Roger smiled at Tyler's remark, then said, "Well, if you're going to get down that ramp and onto a plane to China there are some things you need to learn first. Follow me."

Roger led Tyler and Abby into a room filled with six handicapped men. Pulling up a chair for Abby, Roger said, "Here you go. You and Tyler can sit here. Lori, this is Tyler and Abby. I'll be back for them in an hour."

Abby was wide-eyed as she scanned the room. *What am I going to do in here for an hour?*

"Thank you Roger." Lori said as he left the room.

"Well, gentlemen and Abby, for the next hour you're going to learn how to compartmentalize critical routines of a paraplegic— dressing, skin care, and how to manage the elimination of your bladder and bowels."

"Now, as you know, you have no control of your bladder.

Tyler looked at Abby and smiled that fiendish smile of the ten-year-old boy who watched her reach into her backpack where he'd put a cockroach.

"So, of the three methods, patients prefer the self-catheterization packet that they can empty every four hours. I'm going to pass out an SC Packet to each of you and then demonstrate how to use it."

Abby looked at Tyler mischievously and asked, "Would you like me to help you, here, in front of the group?" Her satisfaction was Tyler's reflex to cover his family jewels and scan the room to see if anybody heard what she said.

To Abby's relief, each patient didn't have to practice. Lori simply used slides to demonstrate the process.

"Any questions? Very well, let's move on to bowel elimination procedures."

Oh, God. Do I need to be here for this?

"Abby, dear."

"Ah, Yes?" She replied nervously, wondering what the instructor wanted her to do.

"Honey, you won't need to stay for this if you don't want to."

Abby was up on her feet quickly, patting Tyler on the head. "Sorry I can't stay to watch."

"Oh, thank you so much." he said wiping her hand off his head. "You're so thoughtful."

Finally, Abby had time to get back to business. As soon as she reached their apartment she booted up her computer and dove into another follow-up article about the massacre.

It Takes A Village

My friend is now a paraplegic undergoing medical and therapeutic treatment. Housed at Craig Hospital, our introduction to his support Team the first day was simply overwhelming. Eighteen professionals are assigned to his care. Yes, eighteen, which includes doctors and nurses who cover cardiac and respiratory treatment, as well as pain management. The others introduced were numerous therapists, a psychologist and chaplain for mental health, a dietician and a pharmacist.

I'm expected to accompany him to his classes and therapy, so I can assist him when he's away from the hospital. It's a huge commitment that family members and I are expected to make.

***

At his Team planning meeting Dr. Koplan led the physicians and therapists through a review of Tyler's ASIA scores, and then discussed Tyler's plan for the day. Tyler was encouraged to participate in planning and scheduling his rehab, but he had no clue what to say or do.

"The Team's goal is to lead Tyler to his maximum recovery," Dr. Koplan said, "to regain his ability and nurture his independence through his music, art, and entertaining children.

"Today," Dr. Koplan said to Tyler, "the morning will include stretching, and wheel chair class."

Too bad Abby will miss my wheelchair class. I'd better show her tomorrow if I want to live.

"After lunch, Tyler, we're going to introduce you to the tilt table."

Tyler looked at Roger out the corner of his eye and grinned, "Do I have a choice?"

"That's what I like about you Tyler," Roger said, "you're willing to try anything. Off we go. Let's see what you can do."

Stretching was becoming routine. Wheelchair class was all mechanical. Breaking down the chair so he could eventually transfer into a car and drive, then put it back together again. "Later on," Roger said, "there'll be maneuvers to learn."

I don't think anyone would appreciate me saying this, but my chair is like having a pet. It constantly needs attention. At least it doesn't have to go out to poop or pee.

Luckily, class was over before Tyler had any more weird thoughts about his chair. The tilt table was a whole new story.

"Okay, Tyler this is the tilt table," Roger said as they walked up to the contraption.

"One of the first things it does for you is improve the circulation to those legs of yours, the ones that just hang around on your wheelchair. We start out flat, but strap you in so you don't fall when we raise you to a standing position. We'll do brief intervals today, but later on you'll stay up longer. Any questions?"

82

"Yes," Tyler said, "Why's that bucket beside the table."

"Oh, that's the 'barf' bucket. If you get dizzy and need to upchuck, you can use the bucket."

Tyler's eyes popped with surprise, "Really, Roger?"

"It happens."

And it did, requiring Tyler to shower and change before weight training.

CHAPTER 15

The next morning Abby came out of the bathroom and knocked on Tyler's bedroom door.

"Come on, you're going to be late."

She had just finished her hair when she worried she hadn't heard Tyler yet. Banging on his door a little harder she raised her voice, "Damn it Tyler, come on. You're almost out of time to get ready."

Dressed and ready to go, she simply had to impose on his privacy and enter his room. It felt a little weird with the lights off and the drapes pulled. Very dark.

"Tyler, didn't you hear me. You've got to get up and get ready."

Lying on his stomach with his head buried in the pillow he mumbled, "You go without me. I'm not going today."

Abby sat on the edge of his bed. "Well, why would I go if you don't go to therapy? Come on, it'll be okay if we're late."

Tyler rolled up on his elbow so he could see her, "What's the point? I was crippled when I got here, and I'll be crippled when I leave. It's a farce thinking that all of their activities, doctors and therapists are going to help me walk. I'm just wasting time and money, not to mention my energy. I'm done Abby. You can check out anytime."

So there, Abby! I guess you've been thrown in with all the other things he's mad at. Well, he's obviously depressed and needs help. I'm going to the Team meeting to talk with the counselor.

Tyler's absence was noticed, but the Team meeting went on as usual. Tyler's progress was discussed, as well as concern for his absence. All were dismissed except for Abby. Dr. Koplan and counselor Ian Lichting wanted to discuss Tyler's absence.

***

Abby led the counselor into their apartment and showed him to Tyler's room. Tapping on the door, the counselor asked, "Tyler, may I come in?"

Lying on his stomach with his face in the pillow he mumbled, "Suit yourself."

Dr. Lichting quietly observed Tyler without saying a word. Eventually Tyler growled, "Well, watta' ya want?"

"I'm trying to understand why you would be so inconsiderate to Abby. She's devoted so much of her time to your care and support. It must really hurt her to have you turn your back on her like this."

"She's tough. I'm not doing anything to hurt her."

"Oh, you've been blind and insensitive my friend."

Tyler rolled onto his side. "So you think I'm insensitive?"

"Yes. It's obvious that Abby's emotionally involved in your relationship. Many of us see it, but no, not you. You're too busy wallowing in your self-pity, and the hopelessness you've created, to

86

observe what she does for you; how she feels about you. She could have gone to work and let you wallow in your doom and gloom, but she didn't. She sought help."

"So, what do you want me to do about it, huh?"

"Get off your butt and get back to work. Show her what you can do. Let her know what she's done for you has been worthwhile. Letting her know you love her wouldn't hurt either."

"I think you're going overboard, now. I've told her our future together is over, as far as I'm concerned. It's not going to happen. But I will go to my one o'clock class. Just keep this mushy stuff to yourself, okay?"

Dr. Lichting rose from the chair and hesitated at the door. Looking back at Tyler he said, "Yes, if that's the way you want it."

***

After lunch Tyler showed up for his wheel chair class. He lined up with other wheelchair-bound patients and listened to the instructor standing before them.

"Today we're going to work on maneuvering your wheel chairs. You'll practice going over uneven surfaces and navigating curbs. Many of you have mobile partners, so I'll get around to those of you who don't."

While the instructor was working with another patient, Tyler tried to negotiate a practice barrier, struggled mounting it, and tipped his chair over. He threw out a straight arm to reach the floor and stop the chair, but his butt slipped out of the chair. Rolling as he fell, he landed on his back.

Trishana, a young darkly pretty woman, about 25 years old, was helping her wheelchair-bound brother nearby. She rushed over to him.

"Oh, my. I'm Trishana. Please let me help you."

She took his arm and helped Tyler sit up.

Strong for a girl.

"Here's your chair, Tyler," she said. Let me lock it for you. Can you get back on with my help?"

"I think so." Together they slid him up to the wheelchair. Once there, he grabbed each of the armrest supports and they pulled him up onto the seat.

"Whew! Thanks for your help, Trishana. I didn't mean to pull you away from your husband."

Trishana wrinkled her nose, saying "Oh, please don't give me a nightmare! That's my brother!"

Tyler and Trishana shared a laugh as he got settled back into the seat of his wheelchair.

"I saw you with your pretty wife. Where is she? Did she have to leave?"

"Now you're giving me nightmares. She's just my friend; my best friend."

"I got the feeling it wouldn't be a nightmare to have such a pretty wife."

"No, I meant it would be a nightmare for her."

Trichina's face lit up. "Oh, I see! You're not married then?"

Tyler chuckled at Trishana's surprise. "No, Trishana, I'm not married, I'm not dating, and in this condition I doubt I ever will."

Putting her hand on his, she said, "Oh, don't be so pessimistic. There are women who will find you quite attractive, chair and all."

Tyler saw no reason to feel attractive to women, but this encounter made him feel good.

Abby walked into Tyler's class just as Trishana was leaving Tyler to assist her brother with his wheelchair maneuvers. Wearing her jacket and carrying her purse it didn't look like Abby was going to participate today.

"What's up?" Tyler asked.

"I'm glad to see you here. I was worried about you this morning."

With a playful grin and sparkle in his eyes he told her, "Yeah, well... it was stupid to think I could miss out on all the fun here."

"I'm sure. Anyway, I can't stay, Tyler," she said. "I've got an appointment at the bank in less than an hour to see about your loan. Can you live without me this afternoon?"

"I don't know. What did the Doc want to talk to you about?"

"You, actually," Abby said with a mischievous smile. "He says your progress is well below par and he recommends two extra months of torture."

"Wonderful. In that case, I don't need you." Tyler waved his arm towards the door. "Get lost, will you?"

Tyler didn't really mind her absence. He could do with a day without her and the therapist both pushing him. Plus, what was she going to do, anyway. Just stand around and watch?

Outside with his physical therapist, Tyler had to learn how to push himself along a sidewalk to the top of a hill, then turn and descend without freewheeling into a disastrous crash at the bottom. He knew ramp training was coming and had prepared himself in the weight room, but it was still grueling. The experience encouraged him to focus on more intense weight training.

After a hard day, and with no ride from Abby, Tyler was tired when he rolled all the way to their apartment. He spread out on the couch and was almost asleep when he heard a knock on the door.

"Come in Abby," he hollered.

Trishana slowly opened the door. "Is it okay if I'm not Abby?"

Tyler quickly raised up on his elbow. "Oh, my God, of course Trishana. Come in."

Wow, is this a nice surprise?

Carrying a tray in her hands, Trishana slowly opened the door and set the tray on the table. It contained a teapot and two cups.

"What did you bring?"

"This, my friend, is a very nice Arabian tea I made especially for you. Will you try it?"

"Of course I will."

When Tyler picked up his cup he smelled a floral aroma. "Trishana, is it supposed to smell like flower petals?"

"Oh, yes. It is."

Tyler expected dark tea but it was a much lighter color. He took a sip.

"So," Trishana said, "What do you think? Do you like it?"

"Smells like flowers and tastes a lot like spices. It really is interesting, and yes, I like it."

The tea was delicious, the conversation enjoyable, and Trishana's presence was soft and warm. They sat together watching a movie and chatting.

CHAPTER 16

In the morning Abby wanted to do something to lift Tyler's spirits, so she got up early to make breakfast. When he entered the kitchen she said, "I made oatmeal."

He rolled up to the table and smiled. "Sounds great. Could you make some toast too?"

She glanced over her shoulder. "Tyler, I don't mind helping you, but aren't you supposed to be learning to care for yourself? If you want toast, you should put bread in the toaster."

"That's what I like about you Abby, you're such a softie."

Not even looking up, she said, "Yeah, right."

Abby turned back to the stove to dish up the oatmeal when Tyler said, "You know Abby, you should get your hair done."

Abby spun around holding a spoon in her hand like a hatchet, and challenged him. "I should do what?"

"Get your hair done. You know, at a salon."

Her fiery eyes glaring down the spoon aimed at Tyler, she asked, "And, what's wrong with my hair?"

"Nothing is wrong. I think your hair looks beautiful and bouncy when professionally done."

Hands on her hips, glaring at Tyler, oatmeal fell off the spoon and plopped on the floor as she exclaimed, "And today I look how?"

"Your pony tail makes you look, well... sporty"

"So I take it you don't like sporty."

"I do. I do. But you've been working so hard I think you deserve something special like getting your hair done."

Abby spooned oatmeal into a bowl and put the spoon back in the pot. She sat at the table across from Tyler, smiled and said, "You want oatmeal, do it yourself. You can butter the toast, too."

"What's wrong? It was only a suggestion."

Abby ignored him.

Later, in a private moment, Abby sent Aleese a text message, "OMG, sharing an apartment with Tyler is like being married! Help!"

Aleese replied, "Come to my place for a break later."

"Perfect" Abby texted; she was grateful for some breathing room between her and Tyler.

In the meantime Abby was striking out in the search for financing to cover Tyler's hospital rehab expenses. The insurance company said that Tyler's policy was an old form of insurance. People bought the policies because they wanted some coverage at the lowest premium. Only a handful of policies were still in force, and there's no way advance payments could be made. $20,000 a year is the most the policy would pay.

The bank didn't offer much hope either. There was money to loan, of course, but Tyler's disability meant he was without a job, which was a big negative. Plus, he didn't have enough collateral to consider even one month's hospital expenses.

On her way to Aleese's apartment Abby wondered about the severity of the situation.

I'm not sure when or how to share this with Tyler.

***

It was close to eleven p.m. when Abby reached home. As she opened the door her eyes grew wider with surprise than she ever thought possible. Tyler was laid back in the couch with a woman in his arms.

Before realizing how rude she was, she blurted out, "Tyler Daly, what are you doing?"

He sat up slowly. "Oh, hi! Do you remember Trishana? Her brother's in my rehab classes. We've been watching a movie and chatting. I guess we dosed off."

Trishana moved to the edge of the couch and started putting her shoes on. "Well, I'm sure you two have things to talk about, so I'll be going now. Goodnight, Abby."

Without saying a word, Abby watched her leave. When the door closed Abby put her hands on her hips and faced Tyler. "So, is this what I can expect from you?"

"Expect what?"

"A parade of women coming to cuddle with the harmless little puppy."

"Who said I'm harmless?"

Abby dropped her hands and held one to her chest, feeling a bit awkward. "Well, I just assumed that if you're paralyzed, it included...

"Not true."

Abby covered her ears, as if she didn't want to hear, and shook her head to get the thought out of her mind.

Too much information! Oh, my God. I honestly didn't mean to go there!

"Well, whatever... that's not the point of this conversation. Your behavior is the problem."

Tyler was enjoying her discomfort, and pressed on. "So is it my behavior through the eyes of a mother? Or, through the eyes of a jealous fiancée?"

"Oh, don't be absurd!" Abby said, storming off to her bedroom.

***

The next morning, just as Tyler's Team meeting was ending, Dr. Koplan made an announcement. All patients in Tyler's class were going to the Denver Nugget's basketball game the following evening. Therapies would end an hour early so there would be time for everyone to shower and change before the bus leaves.

"Abby, I understand you won't be able to join us because of a previous commitment. We'll miss you."

When Tyler turned and winked at her like a little boy, she thought, *Just what I need. I'm scheduled to work while Tyler and his playmate get to spend the night together.*

Abby texted Aleese. "When I went into our apartment last night Tyler was on the couch with a woman. Awkward!!"

"OMG, embarrassing!" was Aleese's reply "How shocking."

Thinking she might have misunderstood, Abby sent another text, "Did I mention they were both dressed?"

"Well, what's the big deal... or are you jealous?" Aleese asked.

I'm hearing that word 'jealous?' again. How ridiculous! I could go a lifetime without being jealous of any man.

She hadn't seen Dr. Koplan approach her. His presence startled her.

"Sorry to surprise you, Abby," Dr. Koplan said, "But Marty Davis would like to see you about finances. Can you stop by her office today?"Abby tensed up at the news, because she hadn't obtained any financing for Tyler.

Well, I might as well get this over with.

"Yes, doctor, I will."

At the finance department Abby approached Marty's desk reluctantly. "Hello. I understand you want to see me?"

Marty smiled and asked Abby to be seated, which she did.

"Well, young lady, I have good news."

Abby was skeptical. She sat up on the edge of her chair and said, "I don't understand. The insurance company won't exceed the policy limits and the bank won't grant Tyler a loan. It all seems like bad news to me."

"Well," Mary said, "Not today. We received a check in the amount of $175,000 to deposit in Tyler's account. That, to me is welcome news."

"I don't believe it. Who would do such a thing?"

"Beats me. However, it's a US government check, so I assume it's valid. You two have a lucky star somewhere."

"Maybe lucky, but strange. I don't understand who would do this? Why would the government do this?"

"I think a thank you is in order. Then, maybe you can relieve a little of that tension you've been carrying around?"

95

"Yes, I agree. But who do I thank?"

Abby wanted to feel relieved when she left the financial office, but it was difficult with so many questions on her mind. Behind her back someone had paid for Tyler's care. Who? Why? What had he done to deserve it? She was terribly confused.

CHAPTER 17

As a woman in her fifties approached the lobby receptionist she almost collided with a young redheaded woman leaving the building. The older woman appearance was neat and proper. Her wig emulated the tight and tucked white haired patrons of every church social across the land. Her print dress could have come from a church bizarre, with the hem barely reaching the tops of her support hose. She stood on sturdy black shoes, like farmwomen of her generation, with laces to the top. She could have been anybody's grandmother.

"May I help you, ma'am?" The desk clerk asked.

An old lady walked up to the receptionist. "I need to see my son. He's in rehab here. His name's Tyler Daly."

The receptionist scanned her computer monitor. "I'm sorry, but Tyler's in therapy right now."

"Where to after that?"

"Probably back to his apartment."

The old lady hesitated, and then said, "That's apartment 4B, right?"

The receptionist looked at the screen again. "Actually it's 14B.

"Oh, that's right." the lady said. "I'm getting senile."

About an hour later Tyler entered his apartment, then stopped in his tracks. He peered closely at the couch where an old lady is lying and had drifted off.

I really need to start locking my door.

Tyler cautiously rolled over to the couch and said, "Ma'am... MA'AM!"

The old lady woke with a start and looked at Tyler.

"Ah, you're finally home."

"Who are you? And, what the hell are you doing in my apartment?"

"I'm your mother."

With anger in his voice Tyler replies, "My mother's dead."

"I told the main desk I was your mother."

"Might I ask why you did that?"

"Believe me it was necessary. I have an important matter to discuss with you."

"I can't imagine what that could be. But no matter what, there's no reason for me to come home and find a complete stranger asleep on my couch!"

"Listen, in a nutshell—your country needs you."

The mention of his country caught Tyler off guard. He blurted out, "What?"

"We learned that you have advanced computer skills."

"Wait who is, we?"

"I'm with the Department of Homeland Security."

Tyler couldn't believe what he was hearing. "Homeland Security? What on earth?"

The old lady was up and pacing the floor in front of Tyler. "What I was trying to say is that 'we'—your country—needs your expertise in computer science."

"I do have advanced computer skills, but so do millions of other men and women."

"True, but you are not the typical image of... an undercover agent.

"A spy?" Tyler asked.

"In a sense."

Shaking his head Tyler said, "James Bond I'm not."

"I absolutely agree with that. James Bond you're not!

"You didn't have to agree so enthusiastically."

"Don't get your feelings hurt. This is a tough business."

The old lady leaned in closer to Tyler. "Look kid, you could go anywhere, do anything, be with anyone and no one would ever take you for someone working undercover."

"Okay, I get that. But since there must have been some snooping around about me and my background, you also must know that I'm in the middle of intensive therapy."

"Of course we know that but we also know that you'll soon be through with rehab and ready to serve."

"Not so sure about the "ready to serve" part."

"Actually there's another significant reason we're targeting you specifically. You have a personal stake in routing out terrorists because of what happened to you.

"Hold it. I'll be going after terrorists?"

"Going after them... primarily on line and on occasion in the field. But your role would be to use your expertise to dig up intel and deep background on suspected terrorists."

"That has an appeal for me since I know first-hand how dangerous they are and how they need to be tracked down and eradicated."

"It's a good deal, too, kid. You'll be given a rent-free apartment and a brand new SUV—both handicapped equipped."

This sounds interesting.

"Ok, keep talking."

"On top of all that ten grand a month and by the way, we paid off your account at the rehab center."

Tyler's mouth dropped open. "That was nearly..."

"Nearly two-hundred grand—$175,000 to be exact. It was a way for us to endear ourselves to you."

Tyler wiped his forehead. "You're making it difficult to say 'no'."

The old lady chuckled. "That's my mission."

Tyler felt overwhelmed by the idea, and said to the old lady, "I need to give it some serious thought."

"I'll be back in a day or so. I'll need your answer then."

As the old lady headed for the door Tyler said "Bye, Mom."

The old lady turned around and looked intensely at Tyler. "You can call me whatever you want as long as you take the job. I'll be back."

Tyler called after her saying, "Will you get a bonus if you bring me on?"

This stopped the old lady in her tracks. "She turned back to see Tyler. "No," she said, and paused for a moment, thinking. "But the nation will."

As the old lady left, Tyler was moved by her last words.

After dinner Tyler's apartment had slowly turned dark. He was brooding and in deep thought. He picked up his cell phone and not wanting to be alone, called Trishana, made a date and headed for her apartment.

***

Abby was working at her desk when a tone signaled that she just received a text message. She picked up her phone and read the message from Tyler to herself...

Tyler will be out for the evening? He doesn't even ask me why I wanted to talk to him?

Abby was hurt and angry at the same time. "I bet it's that Trishana woman again!"

Gus was walking by just then.

"Who's Trishana?"

"Someone I'm starting to like less and less."

I've got to talk to him.

There was no immediate response, to Abby's next message, which disturbed her.

I can't believe this. He always used to answer my urgent messages.

CHAPTER 18

By Tyler's seventh week in rehab he was attempting hand-over-hand rope climbing. Roger hollered, "One more, Tyler! Reach up there. You can do it! Give me one more!"

I'll reach up there all right. Grab that terrorist who shot me by the throat and choke him to death.

Tyler pulled himself higher.

"Come on, Tyler! I want you to go halfway, at least."

Better yet, he should be here instead of me.

***

Abby watched Tyler's renewed physical capabilities through the hallway window. He would have been pleased if he had seen the look of amazement on her face. He had never been physical like the football and basketball players she hung out with in high school. She thought of Tyler as sweet, considerate and caring, never manly. But now, she had to admit he was looking pretty manly. His upper body strength created a muscular physique making him appear buff, as they say.

"Hi Tyler," Abby greeted him warmly as he left the gym. "You looked terrific on that rope. And, quite an attractive build I might add. You've changed."

"Thanks, I'm beat."

She followed him down the hallway "I'm here for lunch before I go back to the newspaper, but I'll stay longer if you want me to."

"I'm in the pool after lunch. Why don't you put on your bikini and join me?"

"Don't you wish? You should ask your playmate. It doesn't sound like you need me, so I'll go back to work after lunch."

When Abby left Tyler headed back to the apartment. As he was passing by the receptionist she stopped him.

"Tyler, your mother's here. I hope you don't mind I sent her on over to your apartment. She's so cute and sweet."

"Of course she is." Tyler said. "Thanks."

Nice to have advanced warning that a Homeland Security Agent pretending to be your dead mother is lurking around.

Exhausted from another day of therapy, Tyler entered his apartment to find the old lady stretched out on the couch again.

As he entered the room, Tyler muttered low, under his breath, "I should've remembered to lock the door."

The old lady sat up. "That might slow me down but not stop me. We've got some business to take care of. What's your decision?

Tyler rolled his chair near the couch. "Apparently you've checked me out thoroughly, how about you? Let's see some ID!"

The old lady smiled. "You should have asked me the first night."

She pulled out a wallet from her purse. She flipped it open in front of Tyler, who carefully looked it over.

"So, you're Elsie Herring?"

The old lady nodded and smiled. "Pleasure to meet you."

Tyler continued to look at the ID. "I assume that the logo on your ID is authentic."

"You can take it to the bank that I'm officially with the Department of Homeland Security... well?"

Tyler looked up from scrutinizing the ID badge. "Your offer?"

"Listen, I'm not here to cook chicken soup for you, sonny."

Tyler let the comment go by and said, "I think I can do the job."

"Fine. Your van and apartment will be ready right away. Any special requests?"

"Yes, as a matter of fact. I'd love a piano. An old clunker would do."

"Hmm... I'll see what I can do." Elsie said with her hand to her chin. "No promise, though."

Elsie picked up her purse and stood up. She dug in her purse and pulled out a cell phone and handed it to Tyler.

"Here you go."

Tyler was reluctant to take it. "I already have a cell phone."

Waving the phone in front of Tyler, Elsie said, "I suspect it is not a secured phone with a direct connection to the Department of Homeland Security."

"Got me there," Tyler said as he took the phone

"When you need help or an answer to a question, use that phone. As soon as you click it on it connects to Homeland Security. You're Agent 11. You'll receive a call back a brief time after you leave a message. Let us know if it's an emergency, then the response will be immediate."

Tyler looked at the phone and then at Elsie. "My life sure has changed in the last few months.

Chuckling, Elsie said, "You ain't see nothin' yet, kid. I'm sure you know that this is all under cover. In fact, you can't even tell Abby about it."

"How can I keep it from her?"

"Make figuring that out your first mission. Oh, and here's your second mission."

Elsie pulled a large folder from her briefcase and handed it to Tyler.

"What's this?" He asked.

"Your maiden voyage into terrorist hunting."

Elise headed for the door with Tyler looking slightly unsettled. She hesitated at the door and turned back toward Tyler. "Did I mention you have to be available twenty-four/seven for us?"

"I can't do that," Tyler said, "I'm still in therapy."

"You'll figure it all out."

"Elsie, is there any latitude for being a cripple?"

Elsie looked intensely at Tyler. "With a mind like yours no one at the Department, or anywhere else for that matter, would ever call you a cripple and neither should you. We'll be in touch."

Elsie opened the door and slipped out; the door closed behind her as Tyler took in the strength of her words.

He glanced at the contents of the envelope and stuffed it under the couch.

Tyler stared at the closed door wondering what he just agreed to do. Did he really care about homeland security, or did he just like the bait so much that he jumped in with both feet. How to keep this from Abby was another matter. Women see, hear, and smell

106

everything out of the ordinary. He'd need to be a better Agent... keeping more things from her than the terrorists.

Oh, damn. What's she going to think when she learns my bills have been paid? She'll expect me to explain that!

A little after eleven p.m. Abby entered the apartment slowly, not wanting to be rude like the last time she walked in on Tyler and Trishana. Instead, she saw his chair behind the couch, but no Tyler.

Suddenly, he appeared as he sat up in his wheelchair. "Well, hello!"

"Hello?" Abby said as she walked toward him. "Tyler, what were you doing down there?"

Damn it. I knew it would be hell keeping this secret from her.

"Tying my shoe," he said with a grin.

She tossed her purse on a chair and gave him a stern look. "That's B.S. and you know it! You wear loafers."

CHAPTER 19

Tyler wouldn't admit it to Abby, but he missed her support and encouragement. He had tedious electric stimulation before lunch, and then the real test, practicing walking movements with harness support. Standing up brought back a ton of memories about life before the attack. Nausea and dizziness made it hard to concentrate on moving his body and legs.

Roger and an assistant attached the harness around Tyler's hips and chest. The straps fastened to a hanger over his head. Holding onto to the parallel bars, Roger encouraged him to see how far he could walk down the yellow and black taped line. Both therapists walked by his side as he maneuvered his hips and body to shuffle his feet in a semblance of walking.

"You're doing great, Tyler. Don't stop now! Give me another step," Roger said as he stood beside Tyler.

Just like rope climbing, with each step Tyler wished he could beam up the terrorist who shot him and force him to do this.

Roger put his hand on Tyler's shoulder. "Okay, that's enough for one day. We'll give it another shot tomorrow."

"Are you sure? How about every other day? I'm hitting a brick wall here."

"Sorry, no special treatment. Every day you have to build your strength. Might as well get used to it. I'd like to see you using a cane when you leave here."

"I don't believe it for one minute. I'll be rolling out of here."

Tyler felt liberated in his chair after they removed the harnesses from his hip and chest. But with his arms still tired from yesterday's hand cycling and his body exhausted from the walking exercise, wheeling himself back to his room was a real chore. The peace and quiet was welcomed, and Tyler's head sank into his chest as he dozed off.

Somebody knocking on his door brought him back to life. Thinking it was Abby he said, "Well, come on in!"

"Thank you!" Trishana replied as she stepped into the room. "And, how are you doing?"

"I'm beat, to tell the truth."

Hugging him around the shoulders and planting a kiss on his forehead she purred, "Aww, you poor boy. I think a massage would make you feel so much better. Right?"

Tyler smiled at the welcome company of Trishana. "I'm willing to try it."

"Good, let's get you onto the couch."

Helping him onto the couch, Trishana removed his shirt. She massaged his upper body and he was relaxed and asleep when she finished.

***

As Trishana left she noticed a manila envelope sticking out from under the couch. Curious about why it was hidden, she pulled the papers halfway out to see them better, and flipped through documents about people with their pictures, stopping at one particular page.

Trishana glanced over to see if Tyler was still asleep, then slid the page out and placed the envelope back in its original place under the couch. Folding the paper, she put it into her purse and turned to leave the room.

Just as she put her hand on the door it opened. Surprised, she jerked back as Abby entered.

"What?" Was Abby's reaction when she saw Trishana at the door. Looking over her shoulder, Abby was startled to see Tyler on the couch without a shirt. "Excuse me," she said to Trishana, "what has been going on here?"

"Not what you think, Abby. He was very sore and exhausted. It was only a massage to make him feel better. That's all. Can I go now?"

"No! This is your doing. Now I need to move him to his bed, and I can't do it alone. You're going to help."

CHAPTER 20

The apartment was quiet, offering a perfect time to begin his research project. Slipping the envelope out from under the couch Tyler set his laptop on his legs, and began to search for information about the people in question. He was able to confirm that the three main subjects were associated with ISIS. The search had been so easy he felt like he was stealing money from the government. Then, came the hard part—locating and tracking the associates who appeared to be providing money, aid and assistance. He turned to their friends, family, and abnormal contacts. It was a tedious business, checking all known addresses, visas, credit reports, and phone records.

Something's wrong here. I thought I had six potential suspects.

Tyler checked again. There were only five pages.

Someone's been in here. Abby and Trishana were the last one's in here, and I'd never doubt Abby.

Looking back at the contents of the envelope Tyler tried to recall which page was missing. He looked at the names and the faces on each page, but couldn't remember the name on the missing page. But the picture; it was a picture of a woman.

Let me think. I've got it! It was one of the operatives.

He closed the file he was working on and called DHS communications central.

He heard, "Message Please."

"Agent 11 here. Reporting a file for one of six suspects is missing. Will immediately pursue the last known person with access... What? I have 24 hours to find it... or, I'll be considered a suspect? Look, how am I supposed to... click!"

Tyler couldn't believe DHS hung up on him. But the message was clear. With a new sense of urgency Tyler immediately searched for the name Trishana and found nothing in the database.

Nothing? There should be something. Hmmm, must not be her real name.

Thinking that she could be an imposter of some sort, he picked up the phone and called the receptionist.

"Hi. .This is Tyler Daly in 14B. I borrowed some money from one of my neighbors. I want to pay him back, but I can't remember his apartment number or name for that matter."

"One moment please," the receptionist said.

"I believe he said he was two doors down from me. Does that help?"

"Yes, there's a Joe Collins in 14A and Aadheen Shekhar in 14D. Does that help?" She asked.

"Of course. I'm sure it's one of them. Thanks."

Now, I'll start with Shekhar and see what connections I find. Tyler input data into his computer. In a few minutes the computer emitted a soft tone Tyler focused on the computer screen.

"Here we go. Aadheen Shekhar alias Muhammad Karim who has ties to a domestic cell."

Armed with a Security clearance and passwords provided by DHS, Tyler was able to access records unknown to even avid viewers of detective and forensics' TV. The results were like pieces of a puzzle, and Tyler liked puzzles. This one, though incomplete, was taking shape like an Amway marketing pyramid. The operative was at the top, and the facilitators, handlers, suppliers, and transporters fell into place beneath. Shams Al Ghatrif was the operative, and Aadheen Shekhar was a supplier. Trishana hadn't shown up in his search yet.

Tyler had uncovered a path to follow, and couldn't wait to see where it would lead him. Perhaps these were the people that paralyzed him in the Starbucks attack.

I hope they are. How satisfying if I could put the people who paralyzed me in prison.

He knew he'd have to work fast, now that he'd identified an operative. Who knew when their next mission would be carried out. Picking up the trail of Shams Al Ghatrif he began searching databases throughout the Internet. First, Tyler located the places he had lived. Then a money trail like credit records, banking records and such. License records were next, then computer and phone records.

It took a while to break the encryption in his computer files, but once into the emails a fascinating name appeared frequently... Abida. Looking up the meaning he found it meant "worshiper, pious, devout."

Hmm, good name for a handler. I wonder if she's in his phone records.

The same name appeared numerous times in Shams Al Ghatrif's text messages. Abida was Aadheen Shekhar's younger sister. With a little bit of effort Tyler uncovered the cell number for Abida.

It would be nice if DHS could triangulate the tower signals to see where they were during these messages. *Wish I could do it here.*

He decided to call Abida's number instead, and see what happened. Tyler dialed the number and waited for someone to pick up.

"As-salaamu' alaykum, Abida"

It was Trishana's voice. He was so stunned he dropped the phone into his lap, but caught it before it fell to the floor. Such a fool he'd been to let a terrorist into his home. Into his life!

"Hello, hello!" the woman said, obviously irritated.

What should he do? He had to do something. "Hello! And congratulations. You have been selected for a three night, four-day holiday at the...

"Get lost!" she said, and hung up.

Whew! With any luck she didn't recognize my voice.

Now he had no choice but to call DHS. He dialed their number.

"Message please."

Tyler spoke briefly, "Agent 11 here, need services, ASAP," and then hung up.

Immediately he wished he hadn't called. He felt stupid asking for data on an emergency line.

A short while later Tyler's Security phone rang.

"Hello, Agent 11 here."

"What do you need?"

"I need cell phone triangulation to confirm the whereabouts of operative Shams Al Ghatrif. I'm entering his cell number now."

"Got it. Please continue."

"The next is a handler by the name Trishana, aka Abida. I'm entering her cell number now."

"Got it. Is that all?"

"One more thing. Please provide a map of their call locations for the last two months if you can. Over."

The call ended abruptly. Tyler let out a sigh of relief.

It must have been okay to use the emergency number. I can't believe a terrorist has been right under my nose... and I almost slept with her.

CHAPTER 21

When Abby came home from work she had a pizza with her.

"What?" Tyler said, "No home cookin' tonight?"

"I haven't got time. I have a date. Could you do me a big favor and shower before I leave, so I won't worry about you falling?"

"Oh, how sweet of you to think of me on your big night."

Not pleased with the news, Tyler asked, "So, how'd you meet this guy?"

"At the bank," she said. "He helped me try to finance your medical care."

"So he's a loser."

"No, he's not! Just because we couldn't get financing doesn't mean he's a loser."

Not wanting to discuss the issue anymore Abby went off to get ready for her date.

She was in her room putting the finishing touches on her make-up when she heard a loud thud from the bathroom."

"Help! Abby, I need help!"

She ran into the bathroom and found him on the floor of the shower, curled up on his side with his face in a pool of water by the drain. She turned off the water and asked, "Tyler, what can I do? I'm in a dress and heels for God's sake!"

"I can't get up. You've got to help."

"How?"

"You have to lift me up onto my bench."

Abby looked at her pink chiffon dress and told herself that it would be trash. There were days Tyler could be so much trouble that she wished she could just leave him there, forever. She sighed heavily, kicked off her heels and entered the shower.

"Abby, if you can turn me around and lift me, I'll try to find something to hold on to and help."

Tyler was wet. Abby straddled him, grabbed him under his arms and moved him toward the seat. The floor was wet, and her feet were slipping. She lifted him as much as she could. He was finally able to reach the seat.

"Okay, one more lunge and I can make it up."

Abby lunged. Her wet hands lost their grip. She fell onto Tyler, smashing her breasts into his face. They were both wet, and she slid down his legs, landing on her hands and knees in the shower.

"Damn it!" She said sitting back on her heels. "I was all dressed and ready to go out. Now look at me."

"Does it mean anything if I say, thanks?"

"No!" Grabbing a towel she tossed it into his crotch. "Put some clothes on."

Later, bare foot and dressed in his white terry cloth robe, Tyler didn't want to fan the fire, so he sat quietly in the living room, as

Abby changed clothes again, for her date. The doorbell shattered their forced silence.

"That's my date and I'm not ready. Will you keep him company for me?"

"Sure."

Opening the door he saw a fairly handsome man in loafers, jeans, a collared shirt and sport jacket. Tyler liked the look.

"Excuse me," he said hesitantly, "is this where Abby Porter lives?"

"Sure is," Tyler said. "Come on in. Make yourself comfortable."

Tyler motioned to the stuffed chair, knowing it was the least comfortable.

"My name's Tyler Daly, what's yours?"

"Conrad. Conrad Gordon."

"Nice to meet you. I'm sorry, but Abby's runnin' behind. We could just chat, if you'd like."

"Ah, why are you here?"

"Abby and I share this apartment."

"I didn't know that. How long have you been together?"

"Oh, at least two months now, give or take. Time flies you know."

"Why are you dressed in a robe at this time of day?"

"Oh, I took a shower. Funniest thing happened though... I fell in the shower. Since I'm paralyzed Abby had to come in and help me up. She was soaking wet. That's why she's a little late."

"Were you naked when she got in the shower with you?"

"Yeah, but it's not what you think, Dude."

121

Conrad got up out of his chair. "I think I've made a big mistake. I don't know what's going on here, but it's not for me. I'm out of here. You can tell Abby to lose my number."

Just as the door shut Abby came out of her room. "What's going on? I thought Conrad was here?"

"Sorry, but I think he got cold feet."

Abby wasn't buying that answer. Her eyes glared. Her face took on a mean look. "What did you do?"

"Hey, I didn't do anything."

"What did you say to him?"

As she approached him Tyler's hands shot straight out to absorb her attack if she got too close. "Listen, all I did was answer his questions. He seemed really shy. You want to know the truth, I don't think he was your type."

"You brat! You have no idea what my type is. Damn it! You did something. I know you did. Next time I have a date I'm locking you in your room!"

She turned and stormed back into her room, "I can't believe I got dressed up twice for nothing. Daly, I could kill you!"

CHAPTER 22

The following Friday Abby planned to be at Craig Hospital around 10 A.M. After two months of rehab, Tyler would be in the first session of his final day. He had been so insistent that she attend, she knew it would upset him if she didn't.

Guessing he'd be in the pool, she began walking that direction and ran into Phyllis, a swim therapist.

"Hi, Abby. Nice to see you," Phyllis said.

"You too. I'm here to see Tyler. Is he in the pool?"

"Oh no, he's in the gym. You'd better hurry or you'll miss the action."

Turning back up the hallway, Abby walked briskly to the gym, where she could see all the activity through the hallway window.

If he's supposed to be here, I don't see him. I'm really confused.

Movement up at the ceiling caught her attention. There was a man holding the rope with one hand and touching a bell with the other. Abby gasped when she realized it was Tyler.

Oh, my God! I can't believe it? He's come so far.

Safely on the ground, he spun on his butt toward the window, while she smiled and clapped her hands. She could see that he was proud.

Tyler transferred his body across the floor and stopped in front of a pommel horse.

What is he going to do? He can't possibly get up on that?

Giving Abby the "keep your eyes on me" hand signal, he turned serious. Sitting on the floor, perpendicular to the horse, Roger helped him reach the pommel horse handles. Slowly he raised himself and swung up into a handstand.

Abby couldn't help talking to herself, "Look at the muscles! They look like they'll explode! Beautiful! Simply stunning! Tyler, where have you found the strength?"

What Abby thought was the end of the performance was only the beginning. Tyler's upper body strength was showcased as he did a circular routine from one end of the horse to the other end. The most intriguing of all was his dismount down the side of the horse and sliding to the floor through the bottom, finishing with his butt on the ground.

Abby jumped up and down with excitement. She blew a kiss his way and clapped her hands. It was obvious to her that Tyler couldn't be more proud of himself.

When he was back in his chair he came out of the room to see Abby.

She hugged him. "You were magnificent. Look at you. You're a new man."

"Now, that was fun." Smiling as he looked up at Abby, "Just one more mountain I want to climb... sit-skiing."

Abby gasped as she brought her hands to her mouth, "You've got to be joking. You think you can ski?"

"Other 'paras' have. Roger says he'll take me as soon as the mountains have snow. Won't that be cool?"

Abby knelt beside his chair and took his hand. "You don't have to be a daredevil to prove you're capable, you know."

"I'm not a daredevil. The worst has already been done to me, so what could possibly go wrong?"

"And, that's how you think?"

He didn't reply, but simply put his arms around her and gave her a hug. "Thanks for coming. It's no fun to show off alone."

"And you certainly did show off," she said as she hugged him back.

Getting ready to leave, Abby asked him, "Tyler, are you due to get discharged soon?"

"You bet I am. That's what this was all about today. My graduation ceremony, so to speak."

Reaching into her purse for her phone she asked, "We'll have to move out of this apartment, then. You're going to need a new place to live. Should I be looking for an apartment for you? Do you know what part of Denver you want to live? Oh, I'm sorry, maybe you want to return to Ft. Collins?"

"Abby, just rest easy. I already have a handicap apartment. It's not far away, so I can continue outpatient rehab. I've gotta continue therapy if I want to ski."

"Oh. You do? How did you find an apartment?"

"They have services here. I didn't know about it until a week ago, but they were really efficient."

If she gets too curious, the truth about Homeland Security will be hard to explain.

"Thanks for the thought, but I'm all set."

Abby was a bit saddened to hear this. She felt it was one of those things she could do to help.

"Well then, can I ask a huge personal favor?"

"Sure, anything."

"Would you let me rent a room for a while? I can't move in with Aleese and Sue until Aleese's sister finds an apartment and moves out. Please? It shouldn't be for long."

"Of course you can. I'd love to have you as a roommate."

That earned Tyler a hug and a kiss on the forehead. "You're so sweet to me. Well, gotta go. Work's waiting."

Calling to her as she walked away Tyler said, "Listen, later I'll text my apartment's address and phone number so we can make plans."

"You know I'd love that. Don't forget now."

"I won't."

***

Abby couldn't wait to text Aleese. "You should have seen what Tyler did today on the rope and pommel horse. He is so muscular, and strong and buff, like a new man. He was awesome!"

Aleese commented, "I see. And this muscular, strong, buff, intelligent and artistic man that you're currently living with is the one you have no interest in. Right?"

"Well, of course not."

"Then, if you would please," Aleese asked, "describe the man that would interest you."

"Listen, I'm not going to play your game, so give it up."

Aleese's final text was, "Abby, what you're doing and how you're acting is not a game. You're hooked girl."

126

CHAPTER 23

Tyler left Craig Hospital and moved into the apartment Homeland Security provided him. A handicapped apartment had never really been on Tyler's radar. He couldn't have described one if his life depended on it. Now he had one with a roll-in shower and special kitchen. The counters would lower from regular height to handicap height. It was awesome!

They even gave him a piano of his very own. It had been years since he had his own piano. Shoving the piano bench aside, Tyler locked his wheelchair wheels and began to play. Since it had been so long since he had played, it was simple stuff to begin with, but inspiration drove him to a favorite piece, "Memory," by Andrew Lloyd Weber and Trevor Nunn. When he finished the tune he realized someone was knocking on his door.

He opened it and he saw a woman and small boy.

"How can I help you," he asked.

The woman said, "I'm so sorry to bother you, especially when you were playing such beautiful music. But then again, that's why we're here. I'm Diane Sullivan, and my son Rudy here needs piano lessons in the worst way. Perhaps you are a piano teacher?"

"It's something I've never done, ma'am. But you're welcome to come on in, as soon as I move out of the way."

"Oh, dear. You're in a wheelchair. I'm so sorry. How did it happen? If I may ask."

"It's a long story. Maybe I'll write a book about it someday. By the way, my name's Tyler Daly. Now, you, young man, must be the one she's talking about. How old are you?

The boy hung his head. "Eight."

"Have you ever played piano before?"

Apparently shy, the child continued looking at his feet and shook his head, "No."

Tyler bent down trying to see the young man's face. "Rudy, how do you know you want to play piano?"

"Because I can play my keyboard."

"Would you show me how you play?"

With enthusiasm, Rudy straightened and smiled. "Okay."

Tyler was floored when Rudy began playing "Memory," the song he had just finished. Once he got over the shock that this kid knew the song, Tyler listened more intently. It was choppy but the tune was recognizable.

"Bravo, Rudy. Very nice! Tell me, how long have you known the song you just played?"

"I heard it upstairs when you played it."

Tyler didn't think he heard right. "Rudy, are you telling me you never heard that song until I played it?"

"Uh-huh."

Tyler looked at Rudy's mother with nothing but questions in his eyes.

"It's true," she said. That's why he needs lessons so badly. He has a gift. All he has to do is hear a song and he can bang it out on his keyboard. He needs a teacher, Mr. Daly. Won't you consider teaching him?"

I have never given piano lessons before, yet here is the one person in the world that needs to learn.

"Please forgive me, Mrs. Sullivan, but I've only been in this new apartment an hour or two. There are routines I must establish, and adjustments to make. Bring Rudy by after school next week, and we'll discuss it again."

"Thank you so much for even considering teaching him. We'll be back. And, oh, by the way, you play beautifully."

Tyler thanked her and closed the door, wondering why Rudy hadn't bothered to say thank you or good-bye.

Just a kid I guess. Doesn't seem to be blessed with many social skills. Damn sure can learn music though.

***

The following Wednesday Mrs. Sullivan brought Rudy back to see Tyler, who conducted a little audition to see what Rudy did and did not know.

"Ok, Rudy. That's enough. It's obvious that you play very well, but you have no foundation."

"What's a foundation," Rudy asked.

"It's the bricks and mortar at the base of the Empire State Building that holds the top way up in the sky. No foundation in your music skills and all you've got it a tree full of noisy birds."

"I don't get it." he said.

"You will." He turned to Rudy's mother. "Mrs. Sullivan, and you too Rudy, I'll teach you how to play the piano on two conditions."

"Conditions?" Rudy asked.

"Yes. First of all, before you play another piece of music you've got to learn the basics of the keyboard. You must practice chords, scales and more. Secondly, you must practice at least one hour a day or our time's wasted. Understand?"

Mrs. Sullivan had a skeptical look on her face. "Where could he possibly do that? We don't have a piano."

"He can use this one. I'll give you a key to my apartment. An hour after you get home from school I want to see you seated here practicing. Can you do that?"

Rudy looked dejected but nodded.

"Rudy, look at me," Tyler said. "Every Friday, if you've learned your lesson for the week, I'll play a song for you to listen to and copy. Deal?"

Rudy's smile was his answer.

CHAPTER 24

The next day, on the way to his apartment, Tyler stopped to get his mail. A green envelope with no stamp or return address stood out among the junk advertising and special offers. He waited until he was in his apartment to open it. The contents contained a note and map of phone triangulations.

He opened the note first and read it. "Can you Confirm stakeout targets?"

It didn't take long for Tyler to see the pattern. Call frequency from Craig Hospital was high, and the highest frequency from that phone went to a residence at 15411 W. 17th Avenue in Englewood, Colorado.

Calls from Craig Hospital… the odd way Trishana answered the phone, and now this address?

Leaving immediately, Tyler lowered the ramp on his van and rolled his chair up into the driver's station. He activated the wheel clamps that locked his chair, and pressed the button to raise the ramp. He loved the formula one steering wheel. The right paddle accelerated and the left paddle braked, while buttons shifted, ran the lights, windshield wipers, and more. It was the neatest thing the government could have done for him.

He drove to the 17th Avenue address and drove slowly past. Making a u-turn at the end of the street he parked on the opposite side of the street to observe the house more closely. Tyler read the triangulation map, and had no doubt this location received calls from Trishana's phone.

Did her brother make the calls? If he didn't, it looks bad for Trishana.

Tyler took out his secured phone and pressed the emergency number.

"Message, please."

"Agent 11 confirming your planned stakeout at 15411 W. 17th Ave, Englewood Colorado. There are three known suspects, including one female and one male in a wheelchair."

"Is that all?"

Tyler said, "Yes," and ended the call.

***

Abby was anxious to see Tyler and share her exciting news. Arriving at his apartment she remembered that Tyler hadn't given her a key yet, so she was pleased to hear him playing the piano when she went to the door. She planned to quietly walk in so she wouldn't disturb him. The door was locked.

That's odd. He never leaves the door locked when he's home.

She knocked on the door, but there was no answer.

How strange. He's home but won't answer the door?

Abby pounded hard and long.

The doorknob clicked, and when the door opened she couldn't believe her eyes. In front of her was a small boy with his hands on his hips.

"Can I help you, Miss?" he asked.

"Can you help me?" Abby asked as she put her hands on her knees and bent down to his level. "I think you need to explain yourself. Why are you in Mr. Daly's apartment with the door locked?" Smiling at the cute little guy, Abby couldn't resist. "Are you a criminal?"

The young boy stood tall and straight as he addressed Abby. "My name is Rudy. Mr. Daly gave me a key so I could practice anytime I wanted while he was gone. But I had to promise to lock the door."

"I see," Abby said as she stood up.

"And I'm not a criminal. I'm going to be a world famous pianist."

Abby found the little boy charming, and tried to play along with the world's next Mozart. "So, our next national treasure musician will be called Rudy?"

Rudy bowed his head a little shamefully and whispered, "Actually my name's Rudolfo, but don't tell anybody. All the kids laugh."

"Rudy it is, then. May I come in?"

Rudy stepped into the space between the door and the door jam and asked Abby, "Well, I don't know. Does Mr. Daly know you?"

Abby reached out and rested her hand on his shoulder. "Rudy, Mr. Daly and I have been friends long before we were your age. The only person who's known him longer than me is his mother. So, what do you say? Can I come in?"

"Yeah, I s'pose, if you're that old," Rudy said, opening the door for Abby.

Hey! Watch it, kid!

Rudy went right back to the piano. Abby sat in a chair close by.

She needed Rudy to accept her so he would open up and tell her more about Tyler's whereabouts, so she asked, "What have you been playing, Rudy?"

"I'm practicing my lesson for this week," he said.

I really don't have much time, but I need to know where Tyler has gone. And, when he'll be home, of course.

Rudy interrupted her thoughts, "Wanna hear me play?"

"Well, of course I do. Take it away, maestro."

Abby leaned back in her chair and tried to appear relaxed, while a deep sense of urgency grew inside her.

When Rudy had finished he smiled proudly. "Is that good?"

"Good enough, I'm sure," she said, feigning interest. "How much more time do you have to perfect this lesson before Mr. Daly returns home?"

"Friday."

Seriously?

"Oh, so he'll be home Friday?"

Rudy wiggled on the piano bench. "I hope so, because every Friday, if I do my lesson right, he teaches me a new song."

"How nice of him. What kind of songs do you play?"

"Do you know "Somewhere" by Barbra Streisand?"

"I think everyone knows that song."

"Good. Please listen quietly."

Oh my, he's an arrogant maestro already.

Abby could hardly believe what she was hearing. This brazen little boy was playing as well as teenagers who've had years of lessons.

She applauded. "Bravo! Bravo! That was wonderful, Rudy."

"Thank you...

"My name's Abby, dear."

"Yes, thank you, Miss Abby."

"I think it's so nice, Rudy, that Mr. Daly has a piano student like you to teach."

"Oh, I'm not the only one. My mom's told all her friends and some of them are signing up their kids for lessons too."

"You mean Mr. Daly has many piano students?"

"He will. They're signing up for all days of the week. He's really cool!

"Yes, I do know that." Abby got out of her chair, saying, "Listen, I was supposed to move in today, but plans have changed. I need to see Mr. Daly as soon as possible.

"That's a good thing, then."

Abby tilted her head and frowned. "I'm sorry, what's a good thing?"

"That you're not moving in."

"Why shouldn't I move here, Rudy?"

"Cause you're not married, that's why."

Putting her hand to her chin, Abby contemplated Rudy's comment. "Hmmm, right you are little man. Well, I'm going to look for Mr. Daly. If you see him will you tell him I must talk with him today? It's very urgent. Can I count on you?"

"Sure, I'll tell him."

Wow, stay away a couple of days and you never know what might happen.

Abby went to her car and sent a text to Tyler, "We need to talk, NOW!"

CHAPTER 25

Deeply disappointed she'd missed Tyler, Abby drove away from his apartment and didn't notice Tyler across the street in the park with DHS officer Joe Brandon, dog trainer Mike Lowe, and Chewy a border collie registered as Chewbacca.

Tyler held the dog's leash in the center of a soccer field, vacant during mid-day hours. Standing behind Tyler Officer Brandon and Mike, observed his progress.

"Okay," Mike said to Tyler, "let's take a break. Chewy, come." Chewy came to Mike and sat beside him.

"Tyler, you're holding him too rigid. When you tell him where you want him to go, the leash has to be loose enough for him to move freely. You can't steer Chewy. You've got to trust your commands. There won't be a leash tomorrow, remember? And the microphones will be in his harness, so they won't fall off."

"I get it, Mike. Let me try again."

"Chewy, heel." Tyler commanded, as Chewy joined him in the middle of a circle made by twelve Frisbees.

"Three." Tyler commanded, and Chewy went to the Frisbee in the three o'clock position of the circle.

"Chewy, heel."

The dog sat down next to Tyler again.

Tyler said, "Seven," and Chewy went to the Frisbee at 7 p.m. in the circle.

"Very good," Mike told Tyler. Now you're giving Chewy more freedom. When you're in the field there won't be a leash, and there could be people in the places where you want him to go. You need to let Chewy find his way. The microphones we put on Chewy are extra sensitive, so they don't need to be in a perpetrator's pocket to record a conversation."

"I know that, but I guess I do want to lead Chewy to where I want him," said Tyler.

"I know the feeling," replied Mike, "but in most cases, close is good enough. Remember, if we don't record what we want in the first stakeout, we'll just try again."

"Well, do you think we're ready for tomorrow?" Tyler asked Officer Brandon.

Mike nodded his head and Officer Brandon said, "We're ready to record some illegal guns sales, and shut that place down."

"Okay then," Mike said. "I'm going to drop Chewy off at your apartment at eight tomorrow morning. Remember, you need to be in front of Chamber's Guns-R-Fun shop when it opens at nine."

"Yeah, I remember all that."

"What about your costume?" Officer Brandon asked.

"I have very used clothes that I found among the cast-offs behind Goodwill. Plus an old discarded wheelchair—should that be good enough?"

"Whatever makes you look like you live on the streets. If you're torn and filthy they'll never notice you. That's what we want."

They were loading to leave, so Tyler checked the text message Abby sent during training. "We need to talk, NOW!"

Tyler knew of nothing in their lives, which was that urgent, so he answered, "I'm really busy. It'll have to wait a couple days."

CHAPTER 26

S even the next morning found Tyler dressed for his stakeout assignment. He wore a white shaggy wig and dirty ball cap. He finished tying his worn out black Converse tennis shoes and picked up his tattered gloves and put them in his coat pockets. He was lucky to find the hooded camouflaged coat. It was so beat up it looked like it should be burned.

Hoping he looked homeless enough, Tyler left his apartment. Just as he stepped into the hallway and closed the door, he saw Mrs. Sullivan descending the stairs.

"Hey! What do you think you're doing in here? We don't allow trash like you in here. Are you trying to break into Mr. Daly's apartment?"

Oh, geez, not now!

"No," Tyler answered.

"What's your excuse for being in here? Tell me that?"

She doesn't recognize me. That's cool.

"Just trying to stay warm, ma'am."

"Well, beat it, or I'll call the cops!"

Tyler, smiling to himself, turned his wheelchair around and proceeded toward the exit.

Chewy was waiting for Tyler at the top of the outside landing. Tyler glanced back at the lobby and saw Mrs. Sullivan returning up the stairs. Anxious to leave before she tried watching them, he rubbed Chewy behind the ears and they went directly to his van. He pressed the remote switch to lower the handicap ramp and rolled into the van as Chewy entered and hopped up onto the passenger seat. Once Tyler had his chair locked in the driver's position he pressed the switch to raise the ramp.

That is awkward. Now we're behind schedule. Gotta make up time now.

Traffic added to their delay, so they were fifteen minutes late getting to the Chamber's Guns-R-Fun shop. Parking three blocks down the street, Tyler placed the blue tooth receiver in his ear and covered it up with his brown stocking cap. When his blue tooth connected he heard officer Brandon.

"We're doing a check on you and Chewy. If you can hear me, speak out loud."

"We're here and ready."

"Good, we got that over Chewy's microphones. You're both good. Is Chewy's harness tight?

Tyler checked. "Yes, it's good and solid."

"Good, so hustle into position. There are some early customers in the store before opening. Let's get'em on the wire."

Tyler couldn't exit the van fast enough, so he sent Chewy on ahead.

"Chewy, twelve o'clock, go!"

Chewy trotted to the gun store. By the time he got there two men, both in their forties were standing outside the gun shop. Charlie, the shorter one looked like the man on a Mr. Clean cleanser bottle. His stocky body was draped in camouflage. His tall and skinnier companion went by the name, Butch. A moniker he received when he went completely bald.

A large package was sitting on the ground next to Charlie when Chewy trotted up to them and wagged her tail. Charlie ruffled her ears. "Hey, nice dog, eh, Butch?"

Chewy barked. Butch patted her head. "Used to have one like this," Butch said. "Somebody shot him for no good reason."

Chewy glanced at Tyler as he wheeled past the men and settled in at the front wall of the gun shop with a collection can on the side of his wheelchair. It was labeled, "Give to a Vet in Need."

"Hey there," Charlie said to Tyler. "This your dog?"

Tyler nodded.

"Damn nice dog."

Charlie turned his attention to Butch. "So, now that I've handled the paperwork for these guns, where's the dough?"

Butch slid a set of car keys out of his pocket and handed them to Charlie. "Here you go, it's all yours."

"Are you trying to rip me off?" Charlie asked. "That bucket of bolts ain't near worth ten grand."

Butch's grin revealed tobacco stained teeth as he reassured Charlie, "Maybe it ain't, but the package inside is. I don't want to transfer no cash here where people could see, so you drive'r outta here. Keep the money and burn the damned car for all I care."

Charlie looked up and down the street, then at Butch. "I want the dough, not a bucket of bolts. All of it better be there or I'll use one of these guns on you."

Charlie dropped a five-dollar bill in Tyler's can as he walked across the street to the car. Butch put the two guns in his truck and drove away.

"Good job," Officer Brandon transmitted through Tyler's blue tooth headset. We have agents with subpoenas on both these dudes. We're charging them with illegal gun sales.

With his arm hanging down by his chair's wheel, Tyler said, "Chewy heel." Chewy came over and sat beside him.

"Chewy's microphones were perfect. Stay cool, we won't know who's next. "By the way, we busted a terrorist cell at the house you pegged."

Tyler grew anxious, and asked in a hesitant voice, "Was there a woman?"

"Yep, just like you said, but we haven't ID'd her yet."

Hoping it wasn't Trishana, Tyler asked, "What's the problem?"

"The girl uses three alias's, and we're not sure if she's Abida, Trishana, or Nadira."

Tyler's heart sank.

How on earth could Trishana be so sweet to me yet work with terrorists? Now, I put her in jail!

"We know the girl drove the getaway car, while her crippled brother made the bomb. The head of the terrorist cell and another guy were the shooters at the Starbucks massacre. This cell is going down for a long time, thanks to you."

A shiver went down Tyler's spine. He had been in the same room every day with the people that caused his disability!

I think their sentence should require them to be confined to a wheelchair for the rest of their lives, just like me. It's too bad the arresting officers didn't shoot them. They deserve it!

CHAPTER 27

Customers continued entering and leaving the gun store one-at-a-time for about two hours. Tyler was glad he put the heavy wool sweater on to ward off the cold. Just sitting outside let the cold sink in. Every time a customer would walk past him he held his hand out and asked, "Got a spare dollar for a vet," or, "I need to eat today, can you help?" Odds were 50/50 he collected something.

"Heads up! It's going down now! Look down the street to your left."

Tyler looked and saw four men climb out of a pickup truck. One man was unkempt with a T-shirt covering his potbelly poking out between the sides of his vest. He wore a beard and long flowing hair. The other three wore turbans, long flowing gowns and sandals. One man had a long thick beard. The burly bearded man walked toward Guns-R-Fun while the other three stood by the truck.

"Chewy, one o'clock! Go girl!"

Chewy left Tyler's side and walked between parked cars to the street. Stopping, she looked back, Tyler made sure there was no traffic and said, "Go" and Chewy crossed the street to join the three waiting men.

From where Tyler sat, the three seemed entertained by Chewy's presence as they took turns petting him while chattering away in their native language.

I hope the techs can understand what they're saying, because I don't have a clue.

The white man with the group returned with three boxes half an hour later, following which, the foreigners took out a gleaming new semi-automatic assault rifle. They seemed pleased and excited while the ruddy redneck rubbed his hands together as if warming up to collect the money.

Tyler lost sight of Chewy when a red mid-sized SUV pulled up beside the men, allowing the three foreigners to get in with the guns.

Suddenly, sirens blared and marked police cars, black DHS SUV's evidence trucks, and bomb and arson vans surrounded both trucks.

A police commander barked through a bullhorn. "Out of the trucks and face down on the ground. Now! You're under arrest for illegal gun trafficking."

"Chewy, heel!" Tyler hollered to the dog across the street. Chewy crossed the street and sat beside Tyler.

Officer Brandon's voice was hard to hear amid the police presence, but Tyler thought he heard, "They're being arrested for gun trafficking, but that's just for starters. We've tied them to the Starbucks terror attack in Ft. Collins, and the one planned for tonight. They'll be looking at life sentences for sure."

Tyler's smile seemed wider than his face. "Thanks, guys."

"Listen," Officer Brandon said, "You must be getting cold and hungry. We've done a lot here today, so why don't we call it quits. Meet us at Mo's Sloppy Joes for lunch."

"You want to sit with a homeless man?"

"No, but I'm sure you're going to contribute the handouts you been collectin' today."

"Hey! Who you talking to?"

The voice startled, Tyler. He flinched with surprise and looked up to see a bum to his left looking down on him. He thought he'd dressed down to be a street person, but this guy put him to shame. The teeth that weren't missing were dingy grey. His chest-length beard was gnarly. Worst of all, he had a handgun stuffed between his stomach and his belt.

"So, I heard ya' talking to somebody," he said. "You one of those government guys that's always pokin' into people's private business?"

"No," Tyler said, trying to make sense of this surprise. "I was talking to my dead brother. He drops in to see me from time to time."

"He's dead, eh?" The bum asked.

"Best friend I have," Tyler replied. "Too bad I lost him a couple years back. Do you have a friend you talk to?"

"Matter of fact, I do. So, I can understand you sitting out here on the street talking to family. But, take my advice, you best be doing it in private. Yer likely to be shot, just fer hanging out on this street. Ya' hear?"

With that, the old bum left Tyler and walked on down the sidewalk. In his earpiece Tyler heard, "Well done. That was some quick thinking."

"Thanks," he said with a sigh.

"Now," the guys in the truck told Tyler, "git outta here, let's eat."

CHAPTER 28

On the other side of the globe a new career blossomed. As a rookie correspondent, Abby was covering a parallel crisis over migrants and Security fraught with opportunities for errors.

Abby's in depth reporting was expected to include the ways this conflict was reshaping the continent in consequential ways. As if that wasn't enough, the Post expected her to report on the politics of the European Union and NATO world organizations.

All very exciting and challenging... but she missed Tyler already. He was so insistent she quit babying him and get on with her life. But, things were changing between them, and she was becoming comfortable where she was. Where they were, actually.

I guess you can hear something only so long before you start believing it. Tyler said, "get on with your life," once too often.

***

Her ringing phone broke into Abby's thoughts.

"Hello."

"Abigail, this is Jake Dubois, I'm the Post's lead Paris correspondent. I want to welcome you to Belgium, my dear."

Still gazing at the city out the window she said a polite, "Thank you, Jake."

"A lovely woman like you shouldn't eat alone. Let me take you to dinner tonight at one of Brussels' finest. Say, seven-thirty?"

"Well Jake, you're very flattering. Shall we meet in the lobby, then?"

"Of course, in the lobby."

Dinner with a flattering Frenchman, indeed! I wonder if this is just the beginning of my experiences in Europe.

***

The next week, at dawn, Tyler found himself exhausted and started to close down his computer. It must have been his need to reconnect with the real world that stopped him. He couldn't remember the last time he read his emails, so he decided to check them.

Down the list was a message from Abby. Tyler opened it and read...

"Hi, Tyler. I hope you're doing well. I just have to tell you that I'm having a ball here in Brussels. And I met the nicest man, Jake Dubois, a Frenchman. Isn't that cool? We communicate so well. You know, instead of German or Russian or something. Good thing I learned French in school. Jake's ten years older than me, and he's a correspondent with the Post, too. He's mentoring me in the protocols of foreign journalism, and makes it seem so easy. I'm loving it. This is going to be such a great assignment. Miss You! Give Trishana my best."

Should I give her Trishana's prison address so they can communicate directly? Jake Dubois, huh? Unfortunately, it sounds like she's warming up to the guy.

Tyler's shoulders slumped as he realized he'd lost the woman he loved. Friends—close friends—was all they'd ever be.

***

Later in the week Abby was eating lunch in a Bistro with Jake Dubois, her handsome and sophisticated mentor.

"Abby, you must come with me to Paris."

Abby picked up her wine glass, saying "That's your beat, Jake. Not mine."

Jake leaned towards her. "I was told to recruit someone to help me cover the aftermath of the Bastille Day terrorist attack."

Abby finished her wine, looking off in the distance, remembering. "Paris... City of Lights and Romance—probably not for me right now."

Jake sat back. "Broken romance?"

"I'm afraid the one true love of my life is... is slipping away."

"Ah! All the more reason to come with me."

Jake looked intensely at Abby as he refilled her wine glass.

"I'll help you forget."

He raised his glass in toast. "Here's to creating new memories and leaving old ones behind."

Abby looked at Jake tentatively then clicked her wine glass on his and took a sip of wine.

Paris was a whirlwind for Abby. Walking the streets at night, Jake took her to the lighted Arc de Triomphe. It pleased him to see the excitement on Abby's face as the lights reflected in her dark eyes.

At a bistro Abby and Jake had wine and cheese at an outdoor table. Abby poured the last of the wine into their glasses.

153

Jake said to their waiter, "Garcon, champagne!"

Abby was surprised. "Champagne? What are we celebrating?"

"Your new memories, my dear."

Jake reached over and kissed Abby lightly on her lips. She caressed his face.

Later that night standing near the Eifel Tower, Abby looked up at the beautiful lighted landmark and said, "A perfect ending to a perfect night."

"But the night has not yet ended," Jake said as he pulled Abby close to him.

***

Five weeks later Abby woke up with a start to a tone emanating from her phone. She picked it up and looked at the message.

"I miss you... T"

Abby looked quickly at Jake lying beside her. She hurried and began pulling on her clothes. Jake stirred and asked, "Shall I call room service for croissants and coffee?"

Abby made a face and grabbed her stomach. "You'll have to eat them all."

Jake sat up in bed. "Not feeling well?"

Abby turned and glared at Jake. "That's not what's really wrong with me. Look, I usually don't do this... this sort of thing. It's been the wine and the city and the lights, my new job and—and my personal situation."

Jake frowned, "Not my charm?"

Abby rolled her eyes and finished dressing. She pulled her shoes on, grabbed her purse and headed for the door.

Unmoved, Jake says, "Don't be angry with me, Abby."

Abby turned at the door and looked at Jake. "I'm not angry with you, Jake. I'm angry with me."

She opened the door and left.

Jake shrugged. "C'est la vie."

CHAPTER 29

Tyler was dismayed as he looked at the piles of folders stacked on his desk. Chewy was lying at his feet.

"I'll never catch up, Chewy."

Just then a tone emanated from Tyler's computer. He looked at his monitor screen.

Great, another five files.

Tyler moved a few files on his desk, knocking off a bottle of prescription drugs. The bottle opened when it hit the floor and the pills were strewn all over.

"Oh well. They make me sleepy anyway. I can't afford to be sleepy, Chewy. Too much to do and... too much to forget."

Chewy showed her sympathy with a wagging tail.

By morning Tyler was slumped over in his wheelchair and Chewy was standing at his side, licking his face. Tyler did not respond. When Tyler's DHS cell phone rang and rang, Chewy barked at him.

It didn't take long for Elsie and two agents in black to enter Tyler's apartment. Chewy barked at them while turning in frantic circles by Tyler.

"He's out cold!" Elsie said. "I was afraid of that. They've been piling too much on the kid."

One of the agents said, "I heard he was your son."

Elsie looked up from her kneeling position and said, "In spirit only. Actually it's a rumor I started."

Elsie looked at the pills that were strewn all over the floor.

"Obviously, he hasn't been taking his meds either. We have to get him to the hospital ASAP! He's a valuable asset and a nice kid."

One of the agents wheeled Tyler toward the door as he started to come to.

Slurring his words Tyler said, "I have to get back to... to my job."

Elsie put a hand on his shoulder. "What you have to do is get to the hospital."

"Why?" Tyler asked.

"Go back to sleep," Elsie said.

Tyler tried to sit up but his eyes fluttered shut and he drifted off again.

Elsie didn't want to leave Chewy alone. "Come on girl. Let's go get Tyler some help."

Chewy barked her approval. The second Agent grabbed Chewy's leash and attached it to her collar as they all headed for the door.

***

After leaving Jake at the hotel, Abby decided to catch a flight out of Paris. She walked briskly down the concourse, rolling her suitcase behind her and stopped at a large electronic display of arriving and departing flights. The sign above the display read, "*Aéroport* International Charles de Gaulle."

She scanned the display and looked closely at one of the entries under departing flights.

"Air France 3108, *Départ* de Paris, 16h23, *arrivée à Wroclaw, Pologne*, 23h23"

That was what she needed to know. Abby hurried on down the concourse and nearly ran into a man. Suddenly she appeared woozy and unsteady. He gently grabbed her shoulders to keep her from falling.

"Are you all right, miss?"

Grateful, she said, "I'm fine. Just tired... sorry."

Abby continued on her way. Once the plane was airborne She removed a file folder from her briefcase and read the contents for what seemed the one-hundredth time. She had to know if there was hope for Tyler, and this new procedure seemed to be the answer. Nothing would stop her search for a miracle. Tyler deserved her best effort.

Nose cells encouraged spinal nerve cells to grow across a nerve graft 'bridge'

Mr. Fidyka is continuing to improve further than predicted. He is able to drive and live more independently. The news brings hope to some of the three million people worldwide living with spinal injury. It may not be suitable for patients with more complicated spinal injuries.

The breakthrough represents decades of pioneering work for Geoffrey Raisman, a professor in the Institute of Neurology at University College London in the UK. In 1969, he discovered that damaged nerve cells can form new connections, and in 1985, he identified that a type of nose cell—called an olfactory ensheathing cell (OEC)—allows nerve fibers to regenerate into the brain.

These and other discoveries led Prof. Raisman and his Team to believe it would one day be possible to regenerate nerve fibers in spinal cords damaged by injury.

When the spinal cord is damaged, scar tissue forms at the injured site and stops nerve fibers from regrowing. Prof. Raisman had the idea the nerve fibers might regrow if they had a bridge across the scar.

There followed many painstaking years of searching for the right materials to produce such a bridge. He and his Team focused on the nerve cells responsible for sense of smell because they are the only type of nerve cell known to regenerate. They believed OECs helped to clear the way for the spinal nerve cells to regrow.

In 2013, they reported how they safely transplanted nasal OECs into the spinal cords of three paraplegic patients who showed "neurological improvement."

Mr. Fidyka was a recipient of this treatment. (Fergus Walsh Medical Correspondent, BBC News)

***

The next day, Abby arrived in Wroclaw, Poland. Approaching the hospital, she observed a sign over the main entrance of the bustling, large complex that read, "Wroclaw Medical University."

Abby stopped as others crowded past her traversing the stairs up and down. She took a deep breath and then hurried up the steps.

With help, she located the conference room where her meeting was to take place. Abby fidgeted as she waited alone at the large conference room table. When the door suddenly opened, she stood abruptly, nervous.

Entering the room was sixty-two year old professor Raisman, and fifty-five year old Dr. Tabakow. They smiled and walked toward Abby who returned their smile, held out her hand to them and then... fainted.

Abby woke up on an examination table in a medical treatment room. A woman was smiling over her.

"Hello there. How are you?"

Abby sat up, looking alarmed. "What happened? My appointment with Professor Raisman and Dr. Tabakow! I can't miss that meeting. It's too important!"

Dr. Balinski gently laid Abby down on the examination table. "They plan to meet with you whenever you're feeling better. You passed out. I'm Dr. Balinski. They asked me to tend to you. I took your pulse, heart rate and a blood sample and find that you're a perfectly healthy young... pregnant woman.

Abby was shocked. "Did you just say... pregnant?"

"You didn't know?"

Abby's eyes rolled around in her head and she passed out again.

Later, after some rest, Abby entered the conference room where Professor Raisman and Dr. Tabakow are waiting. They stood to greet her.

Professor Raisman said, "Nice to see you—conscious and alert. You passed out!"

"Twice we heard," said Dr. Tabakow.

"I'm sorry, gentlemen. I'm fine now. I know you're busy men. I came here to see if you could help my friend, Tyler Daly."

"We received the information you sent," said Dr. Tabakow.

"Your friend appears to be a very good candidate for our procedure," said professor Raisman. He's young and otherwise healthy and suffering from the type of spinal damage that we've had good results with."

"Will he... will he be able to walk again?" Abby asked.

"There are no guarantees," said the professor. "But that is one of the probable outcomes."

Dr. Tabakow was positive. "We've developed an advanced process that involves grafting nerve cells that bridge the compromised area of the spine, giving it new life."

"I've read every available report and article about the process," Abby said. "Of course, I don't understand most of it but I think I get the general idea and that it's a possible cure. That's why I contacted you."

"What we need from you," said the professor, "are all your friend's medical and rehab reports."

"That won't be a problem. I'm returning to the states. I'll have everything sent right away. Can... can I make an appointment for his surgery?"

Dr. Tabakow replied, "Get those files to us and we can make a determination whether he indeed is a good fit."

"I understand it's very costly," Abby said.

"Quite," said the doctor.

"But," added professor Raisman, "the Polish government has been funding grants to cover these surgeries because they are categorized as experimental. Tyler would have to sign a release that would hold the hospital harmless if the procedure would result in a worsening of his condition. Do you have a problem with that?"

Abby looked down at her nervous hands. "What I have a problem with is that right now Tyler has no hope."

"There is risk involved," emphasized Dr. Tabakow.

"I know," Abby said. "Tyler will think the risk is worth it. He deserves this chance." Abby's concern for Tyler was obvious as she looked imploringly at Professor Raisman and Dr. Tabakow.

"Abby," said Dr. Tabakow, "I must stress that if we approve him for the procedure given his apparent condition... we can't wait too long."

Abby looked at one man, then the other. "How do I start this application to finance experimental surgery?"

"No worries," replied Prof. Raisman. "We'll do that when we have all of Mr. Daly's medical files from the hospital of his surgery, and rehabilitation records from the Craig's Hospital. Send us his signed consent, and that should do."

Abby got up and gave each man a hug. "I thank you so much for giving me your time. I plan to come back with Tyler for the surgery. Until then, God Bless You."

CHAPTER 30

Tyler wondered which was worse, the monotonous work he had been doing, or the muscle spasms and fever he endured lying in his hospital bed. He heard the ping of his cell phone in the pouch of his wheelchair. He could care less at the moment; probably just Elsie who called herself his mother, anyway. She already had a spook sitting outside his door like Tyler was a criminal.

Do they expect me to jump out of bed and make a run for it?

Fran, a sweet nurse who took care of him during the day, entered his room. Mid-thirties with sort of a manly build and the mother of three children, she wore one of those short "no muss no fuss" hairstyles. Soft and sweet most of the time, she had a more stern forceful side when needed. Fortunately, Tyler had seen the stern side only once.

First putting her hand on his forehead Fran took his arm in her hand and paused to feel for any muscle spasms. Checking the monitors for his pulse, blood oxygen, and respiration she said, "Well, my friend. I think you're out of the woods. Doctor's going to be happy."

"Fran, let's not rush it. That goon outside wants to haul me back to the sweatshop."

"Oh, his name's Nick Genovese and we can take care of him..." She noticed Tyler's phone pinging again.

"Tyler, do you want me to retrieve it for you?"

He shook his head. "No. Probably nothing anyway."

"Tyler, how could you know? You're in the hospital. Are you going to ignore someone who wants to wish you well?"

"Okay, okay. Hand it over."

Fran retrieved the phone from his wheelchair's pouch and handed it to him. Tyler couldn't believe his eyes.

Abby's text read, "Tyler, I need to see you. I'm in Denver. Your apartment's locked. Where are you?"

"Ah-ha," Fran said with a sparkle in her eyes, "It's important isn't it?"

Tyler handed her his phone. "Will you do me a favor and answer this text with the name and address of this hospital. A very close friend wants to visit me."

Fran looked at the phone, grinned and said, "A woman named Abby? We'd better get her over here, pronto."

As she prepared the text for Abby, Tyler overheard Agent Nick Genovese talking on his radio.

"Yes, he just got the message. She'll be here soon."

Tyler fumed at the invasion of his privacy, and the assumption by the Department of Homeland Security that they could control his life.

**

To Abby's relief she received a response from her text. "University of Colorado Hospital, Aurora."

She left Tyler's apartment building immediately, entered her rental car, and drove off to the hospital. As she pulled away from the curb, a man across the street started his black Chevy Tahoe and followed her.

Getting directions from the hospital information center Abby preceded to Tyler's room. Her face wrought with worry, she hurried down the hallway and started to enter his room but was stopped by Nick Genovese, a big muscular man, who stood and blocked her way.

"Excuse me, I'm here to see Tyler Daly. I was told he was taken here because of an emergency."

"Who are you?" Nick asked.

"Who are you?! His bodyguard?"

Blocking the doorway, Nick said, "As a matter of fact I am. I repeat, who are you?"

"My name is Abby Porter. I'm...

"Abby Porter? The name that he repeats incessantly in his sleep?"

Abby smiled. "Really?"

Nick was shaking his head. "Yes, and it's annoying."

Abby was all smiles. "Not to me. So, what's wrong with him?"

Nick looked annoyed by her questions. "I'm not a doctor."

"I know... you're a bodyguard."

"From what I hear tell, it's exhaustion. They work all the agents too hard."

Abby was surprised. "Agents? Can I ask why Tyler has a bodyguard?"

Still blocking the entrance to Tyler's room Nick said, "DHS regulations."

"I don't get it," Abby said. "DHS regulations—agents—bodyguards! I feel like I've fallen down the rabbit hole. Can I please see him?"

"Go ahead. Maybe he'll stop calling out your name after he sees you."

Tyler had drifted off. Abby sat at his bedside and gently tugged on his arm. Tyler woke with a start. He smiled when he saw Abby sitting next to him.

"Abby, I thought... I wondered if I'd ever see you again."

Quietly she said, "I wasn't sure you wanted to see me again."

"Of course I do."

Abby checked the doorway to see where Nick was, and then spoke quietly. "Listen, we can straighten all this out later. We have to get you out of here."

"I don't want to go back to work, Abby. I can't take it. It's a sweatshop."

"Tyler, you won't be going back to a sweatshop. You'll be going to Poland."

Tyler was so surprised his response was to blurt out, "Poland?"

"Shhh!" Abby looked around to see if anybody overheard him, then whispered, "I'll tell you all about it. But first what's with the DHS and agent talk?"

"Sorry I couldn't tell you before, but I was recruited by the Department of Homeland Security to be an agent in its IT and undercover units. That's who paid the hospital bills."

Abby sat back. "Wow! Undercover? You'll have to fill me in later."

"By the way," he said, "I was instrumental in tracking down the terrorist cell behind the Starbucks attack."

Abby smiled widely. "Karma's a bitch! Now let me tell you why we have to get out of here and be on our way to Poland."

She continually checked to see if Nick or anyone else was eves dropping. In a low voice she said, "First of all, I found all your medical records and sent them off to two doctors in Poland I met with, and they are scheduling you for surgery as we speak."

A smile began to stretch across Tyler's face.

Nick peeked his head in the room for a moment.

Abby whispered, "I think he's been listening. Come on, let's find some privacy."

She helped Tyler out of bed and onto his wheelchair. They went into his bathroom. Abby scrunched up on the toilet seat; Tyler's wheelchair was rolled back into the shower stall. They were talking quietly.

"So, you were saying the doctors said I'll be a good candidate for their procedure?"

"They said you'd be perfect."

"And I could... could maybe walk again?"

"There are no guarantees, however, they've had great success. They're excited about you because you're a textbook case. That's why they're willing to move you up in line."

Tyler took it all in, overwhelmed and emotional; he looked down at his lifeless legs.

Reluctantly, Abby said, "You'll have to resign from the DHS."

That got Tyler's attention. "I'm afraid it's not that easy. I had to sign on the dotted line just like joining the army. If I'm AWOL, it could mean jail time. I don't know what it would take to get out of it but I know it would take months, even a year."

"Tyler, we don't have months or a year. The doctors stressed that you need to have the surgery as soon as possible. Apparently, with your type of injury there's a point of no return.

"Elsie will kill me!"

Abby was squirmed on the toilet seat. "Elsie? Another woman you haven't told me about?"

"She's my quasi-mother. Another long story for later."

"Tyler, we have to go and just leave everything behind."

He thought for a minute, and finally responded, "Then we'll need forged passports or they'll be able to track us. I know of a rather shady place where I'm sure we could get a lead to find forged passports. It's called the Chamber's Guns-R-Fun Shop.

"Chamber's Guns-R-Fun Shop? My God! What kind of a life have you been leading, Tyler Daly?"

"How 'bout you? What about your job? How was Brussels?"

Abby averted Tyler's eyes. "I quit my job and Brussels... it was interesting. I thought you were involved with Trishana and that it was over for us. I got involved with this fellow reporter—it was a big mistake and—I'm pregnant.

Tyler's eyes widened with surprise, his mouth agape for a moment. "Uh... what... what about the guy?"

"I'm not interested in him. I didn't even tell him about it."

Tyler nodded, "Good! I don't mean 'good.' I... uh... mean... the baby does need a father.

Abby smiled. "Any ideas?"

Just then Nick stuck his head in the bathroom door.

"What are you two doing in here?"

170

Abby turned on the toilet seat to face Nick. "We wanted some privacy."

"Honestly! In a cramped hospital bathroom?" Tyler could hear the sarcasm as Nick continued, "How romantic! Listen Tyler, I just got word that you're being released."

That surprised Tyler. "I am?"

"Yeah, you'll be back on the job tomorrow. Elsie gave me instructions to take you to the Dorm for a special project.

Abby's jaw dropped and Tyler looked confused. "What's the 'Dorm'?"

Nick leaned against the doorframe, and said, "It's a covert operation where a crew of agents work twelve on and twelve off. You'll just sleep there, won't have a life. Elsie said the only thing that's worse than the Dorm is prison."

Abby and Tyler look at each other, horrified.

"They're starting the paperwork now, Nick said. So you'll probably you'll be outta here tomorrow morning.

Nick turned and left them alone in the bathroom.

Abby knew what she had to do. "Tyler, I'm going to call the doctors in Poland and ask them to schedule you for surgery right away. I'll go get the passports. We'll need to leave from here, head right to the airport and ditch Nick."

Tyler looked at her and Abby knew what he was thinking.

We have so little time to get forged passports.

A quick kiss goodbye and Abby left the hospital. She had to be at Chamber's Guns-R-Fun store before closing time. If she didn't hurry they'd be behind the eight ball.

171

CHAPTER 31

A bby shivered with a cold fear when she saw the gun store and its surroundings. Tyler couldn't have sent her to a seedier part of town. The homeless men and drunks on the streets made her tremble.

Well, this has to be done. I hope I'm not wasting my time. Here goes.

A big intimidating man greeted her in the store.

"They call me Tiny. What can I do for you little lady? Are you looking for a man, or a gun to get rid of one?"

Abby quickly scanned the room to see if someone else could wait on her. No luck. The man's baldhead contrasted sharply with his long stringy white mustache and a beard that reached his belt buckle. He had so many tattoos it took a minute for Abby to realize under a leather Harley Davidson vest he was shirtless,

"I, ah, want to look at a handgun, please," she said.

"Well, there are over 300 in stock here. Why don't you pick out a pretty one for yourself?"

Abby had no time to lose. With her head down, seemingly looking at guns, she said, "I plan to leave here with the cheapest handgun you have, and information about how to get a forged passport by tomorrow morning." Looking up at the so-called Tiny she asked, "Any idea how I could do that?"

"That's a helluva question to ask. I run a gun shop here, not an underground passport operation." Abby stood up and addressed the Tiny. "I'm sorry, sir. A friend of mine told me you were in touch with a lot of talented people. Forgive my mistake."

Abby turned her back and headed for the door at a moderately slow pace. She wanted to give the man time to think.

"Hey there. Don't be so quick to leave. I've been thinking and some time ago I heard of a guy who made passports. I think they are legal, but I really don't know. I could give him your phone number so he can call you."

Bingo, that's what we need.

"I'm willing to give it a try. Do you have something I can write my cell number on?"

"Yeah," said Tiny.

Abby wrote her number on a scrap of paper and handed it back to Tiny. "Here ya' go."

"I hope it helps," he said. "Just an old friend you understand. Haven't seen him in years."

Abby began to leave, and then remembered, "Oh, the cheapest gun. I need to leave with a handgun."

Tiny showed her a handgun small enough for her to handle, then asked her to fill out the NICS documents for a background check.

"Wait a minute," Abby said, "why do they want my Social Security number?"

"Just the way it is. No Social Security number, no gun."

"I'm not leaving my Social Security number here for the DHS. I can't imagine what they'll think if I bought a gun."

"Sorry," Abby said. "I've changed my mind. Don't need the gun. Thanks anyway." And Abby left the Guns-R-Fun shop.

As she walked out of the store she noticed a black Chevy Tahoe parked across the street.

I don't get it. They all drive the same car. Don't they know we expect secret service Agents to be in every black Chevy Tahoe we see? They're not as smart as they want us to believe.

Tyler had been right. She was being followed. Now both she and Tyler were under surveillance. It made Abby so damned mad she wanted to let them know she knew their secret.

She waved at the black Tahoe, got in her car and drove back to the hospital in Aurora. She had just arrived at the hospital parking lot when her cell phone rang.

It can't be Tyler. He usually sends text messages.

"Hello!"

"Hello. Are you the lady that visited Guns-R-Fun today?"

"Yes, I am."

"Well, I was told you need official documents for a trip. Am I right?"

Documents? This must be the passport guy!

"Yes."

"Okay then. How soon can you meet me at the Happy Habits Smoke Shop on North Adams St.?"

"I can be there in an hour. Will that be okay?"

"It is. The shop is four blocks north of the gun shop. Tell the folks at the counter you have an appointment."

"Yes, sir," Abby said. "See you in an hour."

Tyler had eaten lunch and was sleeping when Abby returned. She tried to be quiet but he still woke up.

"How's my man feeling?" Abby asked.

"Much better. Much better," Tyler said as he rubbed his eyes. "Did you have any luck at the gun shop?"

"Yes, and I should shoot you for sending me to that skuzzy part of town. The guy in the shop was so gross. And, when I left a government agent was watching me."

"It didn't take'em long to find you, did it? What about the passports? Any leads?"

"We got lucky. This guy named Tiny, the gross one, passed my number to a guy who will forge new passports. He called a few minutes ago, and I'll meet him in an hour."

***

Nervous about being in the seedy of town again, Abby drove slowly looking for the smoke shop. When she realized she'd made a wrong turn, she quickly drove into the driveway of an abandoned building, backed out and headed the opposite direction. Happy Habits was hand painted on the window of a faded white building fronted with steel bars. She parked across the street and felt unnaturally exposed as she walked to the store.

Her anxiety remained as she reached to open a door with steel bars over the glass. The inside sustained the strange, uninviting appearance. In the middle of the open room was a u-shaped counter where two young girls were in a conversation. Their tattoos were in keeping with the large bold posters of tattooed smokers and marihuana paraphernalia. On the opposite wall was a long, narrow room sealed with glass and a door. A cloud of smoke hung over three men on leather couches smoking cigars.

Unbelievable. There's enough smoke in here to choke to death.

A voice interrupted her thoughts, and a gruff voice asked, "Do you want something'?"

"Ah, well, Abby glanced at the girl's tattooed neck. Charise, is it?

"Yeah. Pointing to her tattoo she replied, Pretty cool huh?"

Well, Charise, I'm supposed to meet a man here." Then she remembered, "He said to tell you I have an appointment."

The girls looked at each other and shared a knowing smile. Nodding her head toward the far corner of the room, Charise said, "Appointments are back there."

The orange, magenta, and chartreuse colors of the smoking paraphernalia on the counters overwhelmed Abby as she passed on the way to the far corner door. Her first encounter with a smoke shop introduced her to things she never knew existed.

Should I knock, or just walk in?

Abby decided to knock and waited to be invited in.

"Come in. I've been expecting you," a high-pitched voice said on the other side.

The voice put Abby on edge, wondering what this man was like. She found out when she opened the door... a mole! Small and thin, the man's skin was pure white. He looked like he'd never seen the light of day.

"Did you bring your U.S. passports?"

Abby pulled two passports from her purse. "Yes, one is mine and the other is Tyler Daly's."

"And photos?"

"Just mine. Tyler is in the hospital and I couldn't get one of him."

"Humm! He looked at Tyler's passport for a few seconds, and then said, "I may be able to duplicate this picture, but it'll cost you more."

Abby wasn't sure about costs anyway, so she asked, "What do you charge to forge a passport, sir?"

"$300 bucks for yours. His is going to be a lot more work... $500 bucks." "Alright," the mole continued, "What nationality do you want, and what names will you use?"

The nationality is Costa Rican. Our names will be Miguel and Isabel Munoz.

"Fine. This could take an hour. You're welcome to step out and browse around the shop if you like."

Abby shuttered at the thought. "Oh, no. I'm fine. I'll just wait here."

"Okay. Suit yourself." The pale little man turned his back on her and switched on a desk lamp. Bent over the bench, he worked in silence, as if Abby didn't exist. She felt a sneeze coming on and fought to stifle it so she wouldn't break the oppressive silence.

Eventually he placed two passports to the side, got up, and without acknowledging Abby he went through a black curtain passage. Not a light or a sound did she hear while he was gone.

If I didn't need these passports so badly I'd be out of this weird place in a flash. I don't know if I'll ever get over this experience.

In time the mole came out of the darkness into the light again. Still ignoring Abby, he sat, bent over, and worked silently at his bench again.

Abruptly, he turned with two passports in his hand. "Look at these and see if it's what you want."

Abby took the passports, recognized they were both for her, and compared the pictures. They weren't the same. The forged passport identified her as Isabel Morales, with black hair.

"Excuse me, sir. How did you do the black hair on Isabel's passport?"

"Tricks of the trade. Check out Miguel's picture."

Abby compared Tyler's blond hair on his passport, and Miguel Morales brown hair.

"That's sorta' magical, isn't it?" Abby asked the mole.

"It's what you pay me for, ma'am. If you're satisfied, that'll be $800 dollars please."

Abby put the passports in her purse and pulled out her wallet. Sorting out eight one hundred dollar bills she handed them to the man.

"Thank you so much for helping us out. I can't thank you enough."

"The best thing you can do for me is to send someone else my way when they need a passport. Bye now."

Abby left the room and walked toward the girls at the counter. When she reached them she said, "I'd like to walk out looking like I purchase something. Do you have any suggestions?"

"Well, yeah! We've got lots of stuff. Pipe tobacco. Pipe cleaners. Cigarettes."

"How much is the tobacco?"

"Four bucks an ounce."

"Good, I'll take one package."

Not knowing if she was being watched or not, Abby left Happy Habits carrying a sack and pouch of tobacco to her car. She got in the car, started it and leaned back to let the tension drain from her body.

I hope I never have to come back to this weird part of town again.

"Hey! Whatcha' doing here?"

Abby screamed, looking up to see a bum starring at her through the driver's side window. His teeth that weren't missing were dingy grey. His chest-length beard was gnarly. Worst of all, he had a handgun stuffed between his stomach and belt. Abby jammed the shifter into gear and squealed the tires as she pulled out onto the street.

It was a while before she could breath normally. She didn't think she'd ever get his image out of her mind.

CHAPTER 32

Tyler's discharge was processed for his release early the next morning. Nick Genovese was wheeling Tyler up to the desk for release when Abby rushed up to them. She looked intensely at Tyler.

"I got the papers you asked me to pick up for you."

Tyler looked at Abby knowingly, and nodded.

The Admissions clerk told Tyler, "You're all set to go."

Nick started to wheel Tyler out but Abby stopped him.

"Nick, let me drive Tyler. It will probably be the last time I see him, from the sounds of it."

Nick hesitated, but said, "I guess it's okay. Follow me. I'll lead you to the Dorm."

Abby walked alongside Tyler who was guiding his wheelchair as they followed Nick outside.

Quietly she said, "I swear someone has been following me."

Tyler looked up, "That wouldn't surprise me. Wait 'til we try to shake them at the airport."

"Why is this so spy vs. spy?"

"Agents like me, we know a lot... we know too much. They don't want us out of their clutches."

Abby shook her head in dismay. It was all so foreign to her.

Tyler and Abby were in her car as she drove behind Nick's car. She had her eyes on his taillights. She slowed to allow a bit of distance between them.

"Okay, Bonnie," Tyler said, "when are you going to make a break for it?"

As Abby said, "Just watch me Clyde!" she made a sudden turn to the left and stepped on it.

Tyler smiled. "Now, I'd say that was spine-tingling if I could."

Meanwhile, Nick was listening to the radio with the volume turned way up and sang along with Journey's, "Keep on Believing." He was singing his heart out. After the chorus he glanced in his rear view mirror and saw only darkness.

"Where... where'd they go?" He asked angrily. "Jeez, now I'm gonna have to deal with Elsie!"

Abby's car was speeding down the darkened streets. Denver International Airport was in the distance.

"There's the airport, Tyler!"

"Yeah, but as soon as Nick realizes he lost us, there'll be an alert at the airport, as well as the train and bus stations."

"Our plane leaves in less than an hour. Your surgery's the morning after next. We have to make a run for it. I'm sorry, Tyler"

"I know you really meant to say a run and a roll for it."

Abby giggled. "After your surgery, I hopefully won't be at the mercy of your corny jokes any longer."

"You don't hope that any more than I do."

Tyler and Abby shared a knowing look as Tyler told her, "That kid needs someone to teach him baseball."

Abby glanced at Tyler. "Him?"

"If it's a girl, she'll want to learn to play ball. After all you were better at it than I was."

Abby smiled. "All to be worked out later. Right now we have to get you to Poland."

Abby pulled the new passports from her purse and gave them to Tyler.

"By the way, here's our new passports we'll need for boarding. We are now officially Miguel and Isabel Munoz."

The airport had light evening traffic. The information board read, "Now Boarding: SAS—Denver—Wroclaw—connecting flights thru New York and Copenhagen"

Isabel and Miguel Munoz went to the head of the line for pre-boarding. Quickly Abby scanned the crowd. A short distance away she suspected a DHS agent was watching. As soon as he saw her he clicked on his cell phone and made a call.

"Elsie, they're boarding a plane for Poland. They must be traveling under an alias. Their names didn't appear on any of the manifests."

The man jerked his head back from the phone as Elsie yells unintelligibly.

"Calm down, Elsie. Just have an agent in Poland meet the plane and follow them. At least we know where they are and where they're going. They'll have to return home at some point—we'll get him back in the fold."

When their flight finally landed at the international terminal of Wroclaw Poland's Copernicus Airport, Abby and Tyler were among the first to deplane. Abby was pushing Tyler's wheelchair, negotiating fellow arriving passengers from all destinations.

"We made it, Tyler. The most important day of your life could be near."

"The most important day of my life occurred in first grade when I met a little freckle-faced tomboy."

Tears softly filled Abby's eyes. Tyler carefully scanned the crowd around them, and saw a man staring directly at them.

Quietly Tyler says to Abby, "I think we're being followed."

"Over here? In Poland?"

Tyler nodded. "Yep, it's the long arm of the DHS and the longer arm of Elsie."

Abby leaned down to speak quietly in Tyler's ear. "You're really gonna have to tell me more about her."

Abby picked up her speed and continued on out of the airport to catch a cab to their hotel.

***

When Tyler and Abby entered through the main entrance of the medical center the next morning, agent Dover was watching them while talking on his cell phone.

"They're entering the Wroclaw Medical University."

"Hmm... Wroclaw Medical Center." Elsie replied. "The kid must be getting some advanced treatment. Naturally he wants to walk again. I feel for him."

"Elsie," agent Dover said, "You usually don't feel for anyone. Getting soft?"

"Shut up, Dover."

"So how do we proceed?"

"Stay on them," Elsie said. "Eventually, they'll have to return to the States where we can properly deal with Mr. Daly."

"What if they try to board a plane for another destination?"

"Then nab them there! We'll work out the diplomacy with Poland after the fact."

CHAPTER 33

A s they got into a cab Tyler glanced back at the suspicious man and saw him put out his cigarette and rush toward a cab.

Why are they still watching us?

The drive to the Wroclaw Medical University took a little over a half hour. During the ride Abby pulled out the documents about one of Dr. Tabakow's patients, Darek Fidyka.

"Remember Tyler, after the surgery and treatment he received at Wroclaw Medical University hospital, doctors say Mr. Fidyka continued to improve further than predicted. He was able to drive and live more independently. And he's still improving."

"I know you're excited, Abby, but all I can see is a re-run of what I've already been through—surgery and rehab. I don't know if I can do it again."

Abby put her hand on his arm. "Now, now. After we're married we'll be able to provide some therapy of our own."

"Oh, no! Not yet! We can't get married in Poland or the DHS spooks can trace it. Only after we escape to South America can we safely get married with our new names."

"Well, if that's how you feel," Abby said with a grin, "I guess you'll have to wait for that special therapy now, won't you?"

When they arrived at the hospital the cabbie placed their bags in the lobby. Getting down to business, Abby scanned the area for a clue where they should go. To her left was a cafeteria. A long wall in front of her was done in shades of blue ceramic. Four cutouts contained portraits. Water flowed down the center of the wall into a long trough at the bottom. The wall to the right looked the same, with comfortable chairs and couches filling the center of the lobby. A tile path between the furniture led to the information center... exactly what Abby needed.

"Hello, may I help you?" The volunteer asked in English.

"Yes, we're here to check Mr. Tyler Daly in for surgery."

"That's easy," the volunteer said. "Please go to the elevators behind me and turn right. You'll see the sign, *Przyzenajac*. That means what you call, Admitting."

"Oh, our luggage. Any suggestions what we can do with it while we're gone?"

"Yes. We have a small storage room. I'll have someone place them there for you. Just see me when you need them, okay?"

"Yes. Thank you."

Once in the *Przyzenajac* there was much that needed to be done. A gentleman prepared myriad official Polish government papers for Tyler to sign—covering all expenses as a participant in the experimental research. There were also waver documents for the experimental surgery. Family housing was arranged for Abby's stay while Tyler was in the hospital and rehabilitation.

"The housing is comfortable, but in an older residence building. I hope you're not offended, but they are more economical for us. At least your rooms will be quiet, no?"

188

"I think we'll be able to adjust, sir," Abby said. "If we're done here, perhaps you could direct us to this apartment building?"

"We're done, but you, Mr. Daly cannot leave. You need to go to the surgical floor immediately... Room 313. The doctors wish a conference with you. I'll notify the surgical staff that you have been admitted.

***

The next morning Dr. Tabakow and Professor Raisman greeted Tyler and Abby in the conference room.

"Good morning, Ms. Porter," said Professor Raisman. Please, let me introduce you to Tyler's surgical Team. Of course you know Dr. Tabakow. This is Dr. Eugene Lazowski and here we have Dr. Kazimierz Dbrowski.

"Why so many doctors?" Abby asked.

"That's the purpose of our meeting this morning. So, let's begin."

"Okay Tyler, the first procedure will be performed by Dr. Lazowski. Doctor, will you please explain your procedure?"

"Yes, thank you. First, Tyler, I will enter the front of your brain through the nasal cavity to harvest an olfactory ensheathing cell (OEC). This cell will be implanted at the bridge in your back toward the end of our procedures. Then my work will be finished."

When Dr. Lazowski had finished, Professor Raisman asked Tyler, "Do you have questions for Dr. Lazowski?"

"I seems odd to use tissue from the nasal cavity to treat the back."

"I admit, you are right, it does seem rather odd," Dr. Lazowski said. "However, it took many years of research to uncover these

189

regenerative cells, which are the currently the only known ones in the human body.

"Very well, then," Professor Raisman interjected, "Let's move on to the second surgical procedure, performed by Dr. Drabowski."

"Tyler, my role is to open your back at vertebrae T-7, the location of the damaged nerves. Then, after the bridge is constructed and the OEC is implanted, I will close your back and suture the incision."

"Excuse me," Tyler said, "How long will the scar be? And, will it be a problem after it heals?"

Dr. Drabowski smiled. "Nothing to worry about, Tyler. The scar will be 6 or 8 inches long, and once healed you'll never know it's there."

"And now," Professor Raisman said, "let's move on to the building of the bridge across your damaged nerves. Dr. Tabakow, you may proceed."

"Tyler, I will use live tissue, harvested from a deceased patient, to build a bridge from live nerves over the damaged nerves in your back—to live nerves on the other side. Then, the most critical part will be the insertion of the olfactory ensheathing cell (OEC)."

Professor Raisman explained what Tyler could expect after surgery. "Once the surgery is complete we wait. Our experience shows that in 18 to 24 months this OEC will reproduce enough cells to grow along the bridge connecting with live cells on the other side."

"And," Professor Raisman added, "the success of that connection will determine the extent of your future mobility."

Tyler slowly shook his head. "I find it difficult to believe that all this will work."

"Have faith, my boy. Have faith," Dr. Tabakow said.

Abby was so impressed with the doctors, and so excited about the outcome she just had to encourage Tyler. "Tyler, this isn't the first time these doctors have performed this procedure. You're here because it works. Now, act like it, will you?"

"I'm sorry," Tyler responded. "My body has been in this prison so long I can't believe there's a way out."

"Ah," said Dr. Drabowski, "it's good to be a pessimist. Your joy is greater when we are successful."

"Well, enough of this," said Professor Raisman, "The ten hour surgery will begin tomorrow morning at 6:00 a.m. Tyler, the surgical Team will come to prep you at 4:00 a.m., and start the anesthesia. You'll get to sleep all day."

CHAPTER 34

For two hours Abby watched a man in the surgical waiting room read the newspaper before finally losing her patience, and left her seat to approach him. She took the chair beside him and said, "You really don't need to feel obligated to stay, you know. The surgery could last 10 hours."

The man didn't move his head, but stared at the paper in front of him. "I beg your pardon," he said.

"I'm not going anywhere as long as Tyler is in surgery. Why don't you go have a smoke, take a walk, eat lunch, whatever. I'll still be here."

Finally turning his head to address Abby he said, "Do I know you?"

Feigning surprise Abby jumped up. "Oh, please forgive me. I think I've mistaken you for someone else. I'm so sorry."

Shortly after she returned to her chair the man folded his paper, left his chair and pulled a pack of cigarettes from his coat pocket as he walked out of the waiting room.

Now that you know that we know, I hope it makes your job harder.

Sitting in the waiting room, Abby was jittery; nervously looking around. There were several other people waiting, including agent Dover who was now literally buried in his newspaper.

Abby nearly jumped out of her skin when she saw a surgeon walking toward the waiting room. But the surgeon spoke to another person. She was disappointed.

The time in the quiet waiting room drug along. Having read almost everything in sight, Abby began reading a brochure entitled, "Escape to Costa Rica." She heard a voice and looked around the edge of the brochure. Agent Dover was peeking around the edge of his paper and looking directly at her. When their eyes locked, he quickly hid behind his paper again.

About an hour later Abby's heart sped up when she noticed that Dr. Lazowski was walking toward her. Smiling, he sat beside her and spoke softly.

"Ms. Porter, the surgical procedure was successful, and Tyler is holding up wonderfully. The cells I harvested are beautiful. Now we just wait to implant them into his back. The second surgery has begun and is going well. He patted Abby's arm and asked, "Do you have any questions for me?"

Abby was curious, "Doctor, how do you keep the cells alive while they do the other surgeries?"

"Ah! Good question. We have an incubator that keeps the cells at the exact same temperature as Tyler's body. So, when we're ready to insert the cells, they are the same temperature as their new home."

Abby smiled weakly. "It all sounds so precise. I hope it works like you've planned."

"We do our very best. We'll let you know about the second procedure when it's done. It's going to be three or four hours, if you wish to leave the hospital for a while."

As Dr. Lazowski got up to leave Abby glanced over at her "spy" and saw that he was back. As soon as saw her looking at him, he quickly raised the newspaper to cover his face.

I'm sick of this guy. I feel like a goldfish in a bowl that kindergarteners press their faces against to see it swim. If I can't get rid of him, I'll at least have some fun.

Abby put on her jacket, retrieved her purse and dashed out of the waiting room in one motion. Hoping to startle her "spy" friend she glanced at him as she rounded the corner into the hallway. He was on his feet in a flash. As soon as she was outside the surgical wing she hailed a cab. As she opened the door she thrilled at the sight of her "spy" jogging across the parking lot for his car.

"Stop at the main entrance. Hurry please."

As the cab approached the main entrance Abby scanned those standing outside, and picked her victim. When the cab stopped she hopped out and approached a woman standing away from the constant flow of people.

"Do you wish to have a cab, ma'am?" Abby asked loudly so she could be heard over the constant chatter of friends and family coming and going into the hospital.

"Yes, of course," the woman said as she nodded.

"Fine, then. If you'll give me your scarf please, I'll pay for your cab ride. You must hurry though."

Abby rushed the woman into the cab, closed the door and handed the driver forty dollars. Go—quickly!"

With the scarf over her head she spun around with her back to the street. Abby watched the reflection in the window to see her "spy's" green four-door sedan drive by in pursuit of the old woman in her taxi. Giggling, she patted herself on the back and got the next cab.

"Is Market Square nearby?" Abby asked the cabbie.

"Not so far."

"Good, let's go there."

Market Square was so huge she didn't know what to see or do first. She'd never seen men playing chess with pawns two feet tall. Old men smoking and drinking coffee sat on benches surrounding the board painted on the street. The Catholic cathedral took up one whole end of the square. A farmers market filled one side, while musicians occupied one corner and folk dancers claimed a corner of their own, as well. It would take Abby a whole day to visit all the venues she saw on the square. She decided to see the folk dancers first, and headed that way. She learned quickly to hold her purse tight after a woman approached her.

"You American, eh?"

Abby didn't know if she should admit it or not. She nodded her head "yes."

"Gypsies, bad." The woman said as she pointed to Abby's purse. "You watch bag, eh?"

While watching the folk dancers Abby was distracted by the smells of food everywhere. She was delighted with the whole scene.

Later she went to listen a group playing folk music. They were in costume and playing classic Polish instruments. The music was wonderful.

A horse drawn carriage clomped past her as the band played. It was beautiful—a transport of white with red velvet upholstery. Of course, the big white horse was very impressive. It caused Abby to think how romantic it would be if she and Tyler could ride the carriage. But, would he ever get up into a carriage?

CHAPTER 35

Afraid she'd miss important news from Tyler's doctors, Abby cut her experience on Market Square short and returned to the hospital. She was sitting in the surgical waiting room when her "secret agent" friend returned. Though stoic as he sat and opened a magazine, she wondered just how mad he was when he realized she had sent him on a wild-goose chase.

A half-hour later Dr. Tabakow approached Abby. "Hello Ms. Porter. How are you holding up?"

"Very well, sir. I just returned from Market Square, which was nice."

"It's a delightful place. You may want to take Tyler sometime. We have two surgeries to go before we're done, but I wanted you to know the bridge surgery was successful. I found perfect locations on each side of the damaged nerves to attach the bridge. And right now Dr. Lazowski is implanting the OEC cells. It's very intricate, and will take some time."

Less than an hour after speaking with Dr. Tabakow Abby's mental and physical resolve faded, and she slept. When she felt someone shaking her, and woke up, Professor Raisman smiled at her. She sat up, wiped the sleep out of her eyes, and felt surprised to see it was dark outside.

"Oh, professor, what time is it?"

"It's eight o'clock."

"It wasn't supposed to take this long, was it? Is he okay?"

"We actually finished over three hours ago, Abby. Tyler has just left recovery for ICU. You can go to see him now, but only briefly. Five minutes is too much, understand?"

"Yes, I do. I'll be careful, professor."

The professor led Abby to Tyler's room in ICU.

When she entered his room it was so crowded with four IV stands along one side of his bed. A machine as wide as the bed, half as high and twenty inches deep fit up against the foot of the bed. The usual heart, blood, oxygen sensors beeped and chimed as well. And ECG lines ran from his upper body to a computer on a cart.

Tyler's pale skin made him look like he was dead, dying, or just plain worn out. Abby took his hand and held it. She felt Tyler squeeze it, which quickly relieved her concerns. She asked, "Tyler, are you alright?"

He barely nodded his head, but enough for Abby to notice.

"The doctors said the surgery went perfectly."

Abby looked at Tyler sympathetically. "You look tired. I'm going to leave now, and come back in the morning when you've had some rest. I love you, you know. You've going to be better in no time. Bye," she said, squeezing his hand one last time.

The next morning Abby sat by Tyler. "We're still being watched, Tyler."

Weak and sleepy, Tyler sighed. "Where we ever gonna go to get away from them?"

"I'm thinking Costa Rica."

"Costa Rica? Where did that come from?"

"I was reading about it in the waiting room. It's a beautiful tropical escape and besides, with our new Hispanic identities— Miguel and Isabel Munoz—we'd blend right in. And Tyler, even more importantly... I found some loopholes in their extradition agreement with the United States—just in case.

Tyler smiled and his eyelids grew heavy. "Hmmmm, Costa Rica, it sounds like a dream."

As Tyler drifted off Abby's face became stoic as she looked intensely at Tyler. She took his hand.

"Dream, Tyler—dream about playing in the surf with our child, dream of running on the beach with him. Dream, Tyler— dream about Costa Rica and our future."

Four days after surgery Tyler and Abby were back in a conference room with his surgeons.

Dr. Tabakow, Professor Raisman, Dr. Lazowski and Dr. Dbrowski were seated across from a nervous-looking Tyler and Abby. The doctors all had expressionless countenances.

Dr. Tabakow looks at the contents of a folder; he passed it to Professor Raisman. Professor Raisman reviewed the file then passed it on to Dr. Lazowski who looked it over and passed it over to Dr. Dbrowski. He looked it over and closed the file. The doctors then all looked at Tyler—each stone-faced.

Tyler's nerves were on edge. Expecting the worst he asked, "Is it bad news?"

"No," Dr. Tabakow said.

Anxiously Abby asked, "Good news?"

Dr. Tabakow smiled, "The test results indicate that there is good news and not so good news."

Abby's hopes were deflated. Tears filled her eyes. She said, "It didn't work."

Tyler watched Abby and saw she wasn't going to speak, so he asked, "What's the not so good news?"

"Recovery may be longer than we hoped."

Tyler was still uncomfortable. "And... and the good news?"

As Dr Tabakow smiled, all the doctors smiled with him. "The surgery was a success. You should be able to walk again, Tyler. But full recovery will take a while.

Buoyed by the good news, Tyler said, "I don't care how long recovery takes! If I'll be able to walk again!"

Tears of joy began to run down Abby's face. Blubbering, she asked, "How long will it take here? I mean before he can be released from Wroclaw?"

"If he works hard in rehab," Professor Riesman said.

"Which I will," Tyler interjected.

"... He could be released as soon as six weeks."

"I'll make it four," Tyler announced enthusiastically.

Everyone shared in a little laugh, relieving the tension.

CHAPTER 36

At the rehabilitation center Tyler held onto two handrails as he tried to stand. His therapist and Abby stood nearby. He was able to rise, but soon fell back into his seat.

"I can't do it, Abby."

"You will," she said. "I have two words to say to you, Costa and Rica."

In his third week of rehab Tyler's therapist was encouraging him, as he stood and took his first few shaky steps. Abby watched nearby cheering and clapping.

His final week of rehab with the help of his therapist Tyler was able to take a few awkward steps without holding onto the railing.

"Hey! I walked... by myself. I can't believe it!"

Abby ran over to him. They hugged while shedding tears of joy.

***

Seated in the rehab center's cafe, Tyler and Abby were having a bite to eat.

"You know Tyler, the way I figure it, these annoying agents will be watching all the entrance and exit points. That means you'll have to walk without help about 30 feet from the hotel entrance to the cab. And then at the airport, 40 feet or so from the cab to the restroom."

"Abby, you checked this all out?"

"I did."

"You're good."

Wrinkling her nose, she said, "Was there ever any doubt?"

When they had finished lunch, Abby and Tyler headed to the surgical conference room for a meeting with Tyler's surgeons.

Dr. Tabakow and Professor Raisman are chatting with Tyler and Abby while Dr. Tabakow signed a document and passed it onto Professor Raisman who also signed it. With big smiles on their faces, the doctors slide the document across to Tyler.

"Tyler," said Dr. Tabakow, "Your release."

"Just like you hoped, Tyler," added Professor Raisman, "you can walk out of here."

Tearfully Tyler whispered, "I don't know... I just don't know how to thank you."

Abby's eyes welled with tears as well and fell in quiet droplets down her cheeks.

"You're walking out of here, son," said the professor.

"That's all the thanks we need," Dr. Tabakow said.

A huge smile broke out across Tyler's face.

Delighted by the good news, Tyler and Abby were able to leave the rehab center and return to their hotel.

Abby heart flooded with gratitude and joy as she wheeled Tyler into the old historic Art Hotel in Wroclaw, Poland.

Quietly Tyler asked Abby, "Can I walk in?"

"No!" Abby said. "We don't want any prying eyes to see that you're able to walk.

"Okay, you're the boss."

***

Across the street from the hotel agent Dover clicked on his phone and made a call.

"They're returning to the Art Hotel."

The agent listened quietly, and then said, "Yeah, looks like maybe the surgery didn't work. He's still in a wheelchair."

Trying to be patient with her, Dover said, "Of course, Elsie, I'll stay on them. They'll probably be heading to the airport soon."

***

The following day Tyler was sprawled out on the couch when Abby came in with a half dozen shopping bags.

"Whoa! Did you bring me something?"

"I did. I got you a dress and a new hair-do."

Tyler bounced up and said, "What?"

Abby pulled out a blonde wig from a bag and a large dress.

"Oh, no! I'm not wearing that dress or putting that wig on my head!"

"Okay, back to the sweatshop for you then. Tyler, this is the perfect disguise. You'll have your jeans and T-shirt on underneath.

Tyler frowned. "So, are you going to be Miguel?"

Abby laughed. "As a matter of fact, I am."

She pulled out a short dark wig and matching moustache that she stuck on her upper lip upside down. Tyler laughed.

205

"Abby, it's a miracle that I can walk again and it'll be another miracle if we pull this off!"

***

On their day of departure Abby and Tyler were in the lobby of the Art Hotel. Abby dressed as a man and wearing the short dark wig and moustache helped disguise Tyler, who did wear the dress and blonde wig. The couple walked across the lobby and paused at the exit.

"Okay, Tyler. Now you have to walk by yourself to the cab! Go ahead... own it, Tyler!"

Tyler took a deep breath, stood up straight and exited the lobby, followed closely by Abby. He walked with a slow but steady pace to the cab and entered the back seat with Abby right behind him.

"Tyler! You did great!"

"Yeah, I was in pain the whole way."

"Hang in there. I know you can make it through one more command performance!"

***

Dover stood across the street, watching the hotel entrance. He paid no attention to the odd-looking man and woman leaving the hotel. He clicked on his phone.

"No sign of them yet."

Elsie was rattling on the other end of his call. "I've got agents at the airport and at the train and bus stations. They might try to give you the slip."

"Elsie, I've been at this twenty years. No way they give me the slip!"

"We can't take any chances. Keep watching."

Exiting their cab at the departures terminal of the Wroclaw Airport, Abby looked all around as she helped Tyler to the entrance.

She whispered to Tyler, "Now you have to walk over to the ladies room which is just a few feet inside the entry door."

"Abby, I am not going to the ladies room."

"Yes, you are! You're wearing a dress, Tyler."

Tyler's shoulders slumped.

"There's an exit at the far side of the restroom. I'll meet you there."

Tyler looked at Abby strangely. "You're going to the men's room?"

"Of course. Now go! Our plane boards in less than thirty minutes!"

Abby spotted a DHS agent standing near the entrance to the ladies room, watching the people entering the terminal.

Abby whispered to Tyler, "An agent is watching us!"

Tyler groaned. "Gee, thanks for the extra pressure."

He gave it his all and walked to the ladies room with only a mild limp.

In a few moments Abby, without wig and moustache, was standing outside the ladies room exit, looking nervously about when she heard a few screams coming from the ladies room.

Oh, no!

Tyler came reeling out of the ladies room, a little unsteady on his feet. He has shed the wig and dress.

"We better get outta here before I get arrested."

Abby grabbed onto Tyler's arm and they headed down the concourse.

The sign over the Lufthansa boarding area read, "Wroclaw to Costa Rica—with connections through Libya and Venezuela"

Tyler and Abby were in the middle of the passenger boarding line. Abby spotted the DHS agent again as he walked down the concourse with an Airport Police Officer. She turned her head away quickly.

The DHS agent stopped and looked down at a photo of Abby and Tyler, in his hand. "The woman has long red hair."

The Police officer asked, "Could that be her in line?"

The agent looked at the photo again and then craned his neck focusing on Tyler." No... the man she's with is in a wheelchair. Let's keep looking."

Abby peeked back around and breathed a sigh of relief.

"I think we were almost ID'd. I think we can breathe easier now; we're just steps away from freedom."

"A few steps is all I have left in me, Abby."

Tyler started to falter. Abby grabbed him to keep him from falling.

"Thanks. You're always there to pick me up."

"Always will be."

Tyler and Abby look at each other lovingly.

***

At the Department of Home Security offices in Washington D.C. Elsie talked to Dover on her cell phone.

"I thought they couldn't give you the slip."

Dover, still outside the Art Hotel in Wroclaw, Poland was looking frustrated and disgusted.

"Look, this is the first time in twenty years."

"Save it, Dover. Write up a report for the boss and tell him your sob story."

Elsie ended their call. She looked off wistfully in the distance, in deep thought. Quietly, to herself she said, "Good luck kid."

CHAPTER 37

Tyler sat in the aisle seat of the emergency exit row, next to Abby. He had a lot on his mind but was afraid to divulge it in the presence of the third passenger in their row. He leaned close to Abby and whispered, "From here on out I want a wheelchair. That damned walking almost killed me."

Patting his hand she smiled at him and whispered. "I know. You were so sweet to do that for me. I was right though, wasn't I? That Agent went right on by us."

"Never again."

"There's no need to do it again."

Tyler watched the man sitting next to Abby. He was reading a book, and seemed to be in his own world. Tyler started a conversation about the weather, where their flight was going and when they would get there. The man reading his book didn't seem to notice.

Confident their seat mate wasn't eavesdropping, Tyler asked Abby, "What's the plan when we get to our destination?

"No need to worry, it's all arranged," she said. "First we'll move into our apartment, then...

"Is it set up for the handicapped?"

"No it isn't, Tyler. They don't have them. It's small with only one bedroom and one bath. I made sure it's not on a hillside, but it's close to stores and restaurants. Oh, and there's a pool you can use to continue your therapy."

Tyler was feeling cramped already. "And, this is what we're going to live in?"

"No, silly. We need two or three months to find a permanent place to live. Playfully poking him in the shoulder Abby said, "Relax, it'll be alright."

"Soft drinks, beer, or wine?" the flight attendant asked them.

When the man next to Abby requested wine, Tyler noticed his baritone voice and Spanish accent.

I'll bet he's not getting off in New York.

After serving soft drinks to Tyler and Abby the flight attendant addressed Tyler. "Mr. Daly, it may help you to know that you won't have to deplane in New York City. They'll refuel, change crew, and fly this plane to San Jose."

Damn! I didn't want to reveal our destination.

"Excuse me, their seatmate said. You're going to Costa Rica?"

Tyler was miffed, but Abby replied. "Yes we are."

"Expatriates, I presume," he said.

"I guess that's what you'd call us," Abby said.

"Well, let me give you my card in case you need assistance. I'm only a bit south of San Jose in Cartago. Don't hesitate to call if you need help. If you don't plan to live in San Jose, you may have interest in my property in Cartago."

Upon hearing the man had property Tyler dropped his defensiveness. "It's so nice to meet you, sir. Thanks so much. We just might look you up and see that house of yours.

"Oh, it's more than a house. There's a house, garage, and barn."

Tyler saw an opportunity. He looked up at Abby, "This may be a lucky break for us."

After they had all relaxed again and enjoyed their refreshments, Tyler pursued another of his concerns.

"Abby, we need to get married right away. Why aren't we doing that first?

"Well, you need a place to sleep, Tyler. It can take ten weeks or more for our marriage to be certified."

"What? Ten weeks? Why so long?"

"I have to take a test at the Forensic Medicine Office to get a marriage license. Then, after our wedding, the certificate goes to the Civil Registry."

Tyler was shaking his head. "So, what's new? Just like in the states, isn't it?"

"There's a lot more to it, Tyler. Registration can take up to ten weeks before it even goes to the Consulate. We can get married, but it won't be official for two or three months."

"Damn, should've gotten married in Poland."

"You didn't want to, remember?"

Tyler patted Abby's belly. "We've got to find a hospital too."

"Already did that."

Tyler's shoulders slumped. "So, what am I supposed to do? Shut up and follow you?"

"Pretty much."

EPILOGUE

Jesus and Francisco occupied the same picnic table they claimed every Wednesday. Jesus was the smaller fit one, looking like he could be a bull rider. Francisco however, looked more like the bull—twice Jesus' size. Francisco was not built for movement. A warm beer and a fine cigar were all they needed with their friendly game of checkers. The Costa Rica hospital building shaded them, though the day was still 'rain forest' muggy. Nothing much changed in their lives.

But, today was different. Their game halted the moment Francisco noticed a white man in his 30's pushing a wheelchair down the road toward them. There was a child riding in it.

"Strange, the boy doesn't look injured." Francisco remarked.

"How old do you think he is?" asked Jesus.

Francisco took a puff of his cigar… thought a moment, and then said "Three years or so?"

Jesus and Francisco quietly observed the white man push the chair up to the hospital entrance. When they arrived, an attendant came out to assist him. Jesus and Francisco listened in on the conversation.

Don Wooldridge

"What is wrong with the boy, sir? Is he sick or injured?"

They heard the white man speak for the first time, "We're both very well, sir. Thank you for asking. I'm here to ask if the hospital would like my wheelchair for your patients."

The attendant was skeptical and raised his hands in defense. "We have very little money, sir. How much do you want for this chair?"

The white man smiled and said, "It's not new. I don't need it anymore. I'll give it to you."

Jesus looked over at Francisco and rolled his eyes. "The man is stupid. That chair is worth big money. I'll take it off his hands."

"Father Castillo would not be pleased with you, saying that. This man has a good heart."

Taking the chair, the hospital attendant said, "We can't thank you enough, sir."

"It's my pleasure," replied the white man.

He took his cane from the back of the wheelchair and turned to the boy. Taking his small hand, they walked together at the pace of the cane.

"We go home now, daddy?"

"Yes Tyler, we're going home.

ABOUT THE AUTHOR

Prolific writer, Don Wooldridge brings his creative energies once more to the forefront, writing of issues that exist within our country; issues he addresses from a humane and valiant perspective. In his Trilogy: *Clayton County,* Don offers a perspective, different than the Government holds, about bartering. He postures it is more a culture than a tax evasion tactic. Deeply loyal to family and friendships, Wooldridge was led to carry on the writings of another in *Bible Moments* and *Yankee Settlement.* He boldly and courageously sought to change the nation's perspective on living with Bipolar II Disorder in *Fear is My Co-Pilo*t.

Each of Don's books is written from a genuine sense of knowing the community. Don Wooldridge, born and raised in Davenport, Iowa, lived in the Mississippi River Valley for over 30 years. As a writer Don remembers the people of the small river communities and shares their faith that small town values and lifestyle will be everlasting.

Don's education spans from Southwest Texas State University in San Marcos, Texas… to Rutgers University in Brunswick, New

Jersey. An accomplished writer, he spent 30 years in the technical training and development arena, as a technical writer, instructional designer, and interactive learning systems designer and producer. Wooldridge's career took him far from his roots... throughout the US and Canada, as well as England, Sweden, Germany and the Netherlands.

Today, Don enjoys putting his voice to print, and using his writing as a vehicle for readers to look at the world around them with more empathy and understanding. He cannot escape his quick humor as it pops up in the many manuscripts he has penned—readers are enriched by it! Writing novels inspired by his heritage and the communities around him, the author always welcomes the opportunity to speak about the varied topics his books cover, and his journey as an author. Don offers his services through keynote speaking, book readings and author interviews. His greatest desire is to share the experiences he enjoyed in life, as he turns them into fiction.

AUTHOR'S REQUEST FOR REVIEWS

If you enjoyed reading *Broken Dreams* I would appreciate it if you would help others enjoy the book, too.

- ♡ **LEND IT.** This book is lending enabled, so please feel free to share with a friend.
- ♡ **RECOMMEND IT**. Please help other readers find the book by recommending it to readers' groups, discussion boards, Goodreads, etc.
- ♡ **REVIEW IT.** Please tell others why you liked this book by reviewing it on the site where you purchased it, on your favorite book site, or your own blog. Amazon, being probably the largest distributor of books as the online giant bookstore, makes the review process easy··· just search for the book on Amazon, and then click on the hyperlink, Customer Reviews. You will be taken to just the right area to post your own review of what you liked about the book

and what you feel other readers might experience. Oh, and thank you in advance!

♡ **EMAIL ME.** I'd love to hear from you.

booksbydon@gmail.com

You are invited to connect with me at:

www.donwooldridgeauthor.com

https://twitter.com/DWoolAuthor

https://www.facebook.com/DonWooldridgeAuthor

https://www.goodreads.com/author/show/5224857.Don_Wooldridge

https://www.linkedin.com/pub/don-wooldridge/71/130/122

https://www.amazon.com/Don-Wooldridge/e/B005IAZZP2

www.ingramcontent.com/pod-product-compliance
Lightning Source LLC
Chambersburg PA
CBHW070619130626
46556CB00001B/412